A STEEP CLIMB

A STEEP CLIMB

THE WAR-TORN VETERAN

AND

THE UN-SCHOLARLY SPIRITUAL ECCENTRIC

Dear Carolyn
May the Holy Spirit
guide you as you
read this book.
Much Aloha,
J. M. Joseph
(Ruth Silberstein)

J.M. JOSEPH

Library of Congress Control Number:		2015920499
ISBN:	Hardcover	978-1-5035-9996-3
	Softcover	978-1-5035-9880-5
	eBook	978-1-5035-9706-8

To order additional copies of this book, contact:
Xlibris
1-888-795-4274
www.Xlibris.com
Orders@Xlibris.com
722609

CONTENTS

This book is dedicated to the Blessed Trinity: our Heavenly Father; His Son, our Lord, Jesus Christ, who has come in the flesh and His Holy Mother; and the Holy Spirit.

Chapter 1

The Beginning of Wars

It began on a beautiful Sunday morning, with blue skies and swaying palm trees. It was so picturesque in Hawaii: placid, relaxing, and peaceful. The kingly, colossal, silver-gray battleships were sitting still in shining majesty on the blue-green carpet waters of Pearl Harbor. Basking in the golden rays of the emerging sun, these giants were unaware of their pending dethronement.

Boom … boom … boom! This scene of serenity was shattered by bombs dropped by planes painted with the sun over Pearl Harbor. Even those assigned to keeping the islands safe did not detect the oncoming slaughter. Perhaps the off-hours social activities at that time affected those monitoring the radar screens.

A frightened little boy ran as fast as he could to find his mother, wondering what was happening. "Mama, Mama, Ma … ma!" he shouted, with tears rolling down his cheeks and fear in every corner of his small body. Little did he know then, at the tender age of three, that he would face similar experiences in future conflicts in Korea, Japan, and Vietnam. Those experiences were yet so remote from his home in Hawaii—too far away to be conceived of in 1941.

"Hurry, hurry! Come into the house," shouted his mother, Ann (really his grandmother who had adopted him). She turned the radio on. In a traumatic tone, without hesitation, the radio announcer loudly called for all military, government, and shipyard personnel at Pearl Harbor to immediately report. In response, Lou's adopted father, Henry (who was his grandfather), reported to the Pearl Harbor shipping yard. As Henry would later repeatedly say, his life was saved that day because he ducked behind huge cylinders in the nick of time as Japanese firefighter planes sprayed bullets directly over his head. And Henry would say, "That's why I'm bald-headed!" This tale was told with a chuckle for the rest of his life.

Even Lou's stepfather, Ralph, who was working with the office of the registrar for the Territory of Hawaii, was called to the scene to oversee and care for the dead. While the family came to grips with what was happening, cars, trucks, and other vehicles raced toward Pearl Harbor down the main access street on which Lou's house was located. In response to a call to return to base, a sailor speeding on a motorcycle lost control at an intersection in Kalihi when the traffic light turned red. The driver and motorcycle climbed a telephone pole almost to the top. The pole then dropped the motorcycle and sailor to the pavement below. Both lay permanently lifeless as vehicles whizzed by—some noticing them, some not. As the sailor's blood painted the street red, Lou's biological mother, Lana, stood by the window, watching in horror.

"Get away from there!" shouted Ann. She rushed toward Lana, who was in her seventh month of pregnancy, and pulled her away from the window.

Lou's stepdad, Ralph, worked ceaselessly for endless days and nights in makeshift tents of death. Lines of tables were set up for piles of the bodies of the dead, many of whom were sailors. Some of the people were from other branches of the military, and some were civilians.

When time permitted, Ralph would return home with the stench of death still in his nostrils. "Gosh," he would say to Lana, "even though I covered my nose and mouth with my handkerchief, I still smell the decomposing bodies of those souls." Although he was a staunch man, Ralph displayed concern for each and every soul whose body lay on the tables. He would pray that these souls were at peace with the Almighty.

Blackouts then began. Black curtains were drawn at night, lest the enemy should find the islands through the slightest glimmer of light. It was said that, during the day, they had received assistance from supporters on the chain of islands in the Pacific. Rumor had it that they planted crops in the shapes of arrows, row after row, to direct the Japanese planes toward the island of Oahu, the target for their bombings. As a result of this attack by Japan, the internment of Hawaii's Japanese inhabitants began in California, leaving scars of the evil of war to this day. Lou did not know that he, too, would experience such scars of war in his lifetime.

As years passed, Lou grew into a typical young boy who was impressed by rituals, with little understanding of them. "Dominus vobiscum. Take and eat. This is my body, and this is my blood," Lou would blurt out with a grin at breakfast time. His sister and two younger brothers would giggle as they knelt in front of a classic black grand piano bench in the living room. Lou gave them pieces of bread and grape juice from a wineglass that they had found in the white paneled-glass kitchen cabinet. "Don't bite my finger, now!" he would instruct them as he shoved the pieces of bread into their mouths. Shove he did, along with chuckles. With glee and excitement, they all wanted to take turns giving out bread over a small blue dish. What humorous merriment penetrated the household then!

"Now, where is that loaf of bread?" Lana would mutter as she moved from cabinet to cabinet in the kitchen. She could not understand what happened to the bread that Ralph had bought the day before. "My, the kids are growing so much they're eating us out of house and lot," she would remark to her husband. The warm days in Hawaii helped provide a reason for the disappearance of the grape juice from the white refrigerator, other than the children emulating ministers in the consecration of the Holy Eucharist.

***

So where do I fit into Lou's life? In my infancy, my parents moved our family from Amherst, Massachusetts, to Hawaii. Lou and I lived next door to one another and grew up in the same neighborhood. We were close as childhood friends, as teenagers, and as adults. People would say that we were like peanut butter and jelly. We were just like brothers. He was the oldest out of three boys and a girl, and I, John, just happened to be the only other male in the neighborhood who lived close to him. We were the same age, so we had a lot in common even though we attended different schools.

The years of youth passed by quickly, and in no time at all, Lou was in high school. He attended a high-performing public high school while I went to a high-performing private school. We did fight a bit even though we were buddies. We played on opposite teams in football. After one game, we disagreed on a play that he had made. It heated up with yelling at first and then shoving. Finally, I threw a punch at his face, and his tooth came flying out. That ended it all. It took time to heal our relationship after that.

While in high school, Lou drove a 1947 Ford, dark green with whitewall tires. Boy, did it stand out! That was the fad in those days: stark, contrasting colors. A dark or solid-colored car with whitewall tires. Wow! That's what most guys wanted to drive.

High school opened up a new interest for Lou. He started to take singing roles in school plays. People said he had a voice like Mario Lanza. You would know whenever he had a role; during practice, his voice would reverberate off the mountain walls of the valley where we lived. His voice was deep, rich, and strong, bellowing from the depths of his diaphragm.

This was the inception of his love for the performing arts and his aim to start a singing career at the Juilliard School in New York. However, kismet did not hold this in store for him. As his high school years ended, he fell deeply in love and decided to marry his first love, thinking it would last forever. A beautiful baby boy was born, who became the love of his life and his reason to live. The real-life scenario had him selling cars and giving up his plans of attending the Juilliard School. It all flowed over the waterfall. Such was life for a young husband and father.

Being so young and unprepared to handle life's rude awakenings, he was divorced within nine months, and he enlisted in the army. When Lou left, I thought that maybe it was for the best that he move on in his life. Henry confirmed my thought as I overheard him say to Ralph, "Yep, the army will help him to grow up and will make a man out of him." It was said that the military helped many youth build self-discipline and grow to become men capable of handling life's trials and tribulations. He was at an intersection of change in his life and in need of such.

Ralph happened to be serving on the draft board. Lou remembered when Ralph said to him worriedly as they did away with the army draft, "One day, America will regret doing away with the draft. There will not be enough soldiers to fight the wars." Of course, many thought that modern technology would replace humans on the battlefield.

As for me, the medical profession drew me to it from a young age. With a yearning to save lives, I wanted to walk the pathway to becoming a general surgeon. I began course work at a local university with plans to transfer later to a medical institution. At that time, no medical degree was offered in Honolulu.

Later, as we took different paths in life, we still wanted the best for each other; we kept in touch all the time, through marriage, divorce, and children. I really was part of the family. We were buddies. We were like family!

Chapter 2

Service to God, Family, and Country

In March 1954, Lou enlisted in the US Army. This was a painful growing period for him. Of course, his thoughts were on his ex-wife and eleven-month-old son. Lou's mom made him his favorite foods and brought them on visits to Schofield Barracks, where he was stationed. He was fortunate because she, along with Ralph, who drove, and Lana, would deliver shoyu chicken, laulau, poi, rice, and sweet and sour pork to him. They thought that the army would never serve these ethnic dishes to the men. I would always tag along on these visits, being like a family member. Lou and I would see a movie on the base after he ate. He really didn't want to eat, as he was trying to lose weight, but he ate a little to please his mother. In any case, these visits were convenient, for they allowed Ralph, Lana, and Ann time to visit family members who lived near the base in Wahiawa.

During spring break in 1954, on one of our family visits to Schofield Barracks and after our usual snacking on home-cooked foods, Lou and I took in a movie on the base. *Miss Sadie Thompson*, starring Rita Hayworth, was playing at the theater. Lou wanted to see this movie because it had been filmed on one of the outer islands, Kauai. I recall the lush greenery and island flowers in many of the background scenes and, of course, the beautiful, blue Pacific Ocean. For Lou especially, it was a pleasure to watch after viewing the plain walls of the barracks on a daily basis. We just sat back with other GIs and their families and enjoyed it.

I've never forgotten when the movie *White Christmas* opened at the theater in 1954. Lou happened to be home at that time. "Come on, John; it's winter break. Let's go take in this movie," he said with youthful excitement. The Christmas colors of vibrant red and white in the movie were stunning, along with the singing of Bing Crosby, Rosemary Clooney, and others. It gave him and me the spark to have a happy holiday season with our families. After we got back home, Lou was seen that evening hanging red and white decorations on every window of his house. He did things that made people chuckle.

Lou served in the army from 1954 to 1957. As time went on, he heard about what the other branches of the military offered, and he transferred from the army to the air force and stayed there from January 1958 to 1961. Because Lou traveled for his military assignments for the army and the air force, his perspective on life broadened beyond the Hawaiian Islands.

In the first half of the '50s, Lou was stationed along the border of North and South Korea. Whenever Lou came home on leave, it had to be celebrated with a dinner. His family and friends surrounded him at his adopted parents' home in Kalihi, close to the Oahu Prison. Ann routinely prepared a luau feast and anything else that was considered local food not found in Korea. And, of course, there were always alcoholic drinks. The ukulele was brought out for anyone to strum its melodious strings. If you could do a sing-along, that was even better.

Food, music, and alcohol were the three basic ingredients of a happy time, a celebration, or a party back in those days. In fact, as far back as I can remember, whenever there were parties, or whenever you visited someone, there was always alcohol. You could not have a party or a visit without alcohol being offered, at least in our group of family and friends. Alcohol in this family environment was a staple, like rice or potatoes were for a meal, or it was a sign of hospitality when visiting homes. If there were arguments or fights, it was the fault of the alcohol, not the human. How ironic! And no one, absolutely no one, ever mentioned the word *alcoholic* in the family.

Even Lou's grandfather, Henry, took to the bottle back then. When he began to argue and be loud and boisterous at family parties, they said he had the "snakes." His alcoholic behavior always interrupted and dispersed family parties. But the odd fact is that it was acceptable. It was even thought that they should let him drink later on into the family gathering, thereby making him the clock, with the onslaught of the snakes signaling it was time to leave. Then the party would end abruptly.

Why wasn't alcoholism spoken about? I don't think it was known or understood in those days or part of our cultural environment, at least not for Lou's family. Alcohol was looked upon as part of social graciousness or hospitality. Unfortunately, Lou's family genes were not immune to it. As a result, some family members took to drinking even without visitors. So, for Lou, it was bound to happen.

As I further conceptualized culture, I found it causes blindness to what is to be in the near future. It's the same as a culture or custom that gives gifts to all who attend a party in honor of someone. In times of economic crisis, when it is very, very difficult, should the custom be continued? Culture, at times, takes over common sense. This is obvious when culture is embedded more in emotions, thereby overtaking the intellect.

***

As years passed on, while serving in Korea, Lou felt that he could afford to give his two younger brothers and sister something that his parents could not afford. He sent his two brothers dark olive-green waterproof jackets embroidered with golden dragons and matching outdoor head coverings lined with dark gray faux fur. He sent beautiful, shiny, pink silk Chinese pajamas embroidered with golden dragons to his young sister. The pajamas had a matching robe, also embroidered with a golden dragon, which came with matching embroidered slippers edged with white faux fur. They all felt like princes and a princess when they tried on the new apparel.

While his sister twirled across the living-room floor, much to their parents' delight, his two brothers raced excitedly over to my house. "Uncle, Uncle, look at what Lou sent us!" they shouted as their feet fell heavily on the wooden porch. They were so anxious to show off their new attire and call me over to their house.

As his young siblings grew up, Lou wanted them to travel in order to widen their perspectives in life. Because he was seeing and learning so much by serving and traveling for the different branches of the military, he wanted the same for his brothers and sister. To move them in this direction, he sent all three Samsonite luggage in dark, shiny brown with an alligator-skin pattern. Each one had the large- and medium-size pieces, and the compact cosmetic piece went to his sister. His dreams for his siblings came true, as they all went on a trip to the mainland when his sister was a junior in college. He felt so proud to be a part of their first travel experience beyond the islands, the fresh opening of their minds.

Throughout all of this, his family would write to him, thank him, and ask him how he was doing. In his usual fashion, he would simply reply, "Don't worry about me. I'm okay. I'm fine." I always knew how he was doing through phone calls made to his family and letters sent home.

When stationed in Japan, he sent his sister a Japanese doll in a reddish-brown wood and glass case in celebration of "Girls' Day." Maybe he did it because his sister was always sick with asthma and the damp climate where we lived in the valley triggered many attacks. The doll wore a stunning red-gold-and-white-threaded kimono, carrying lavender blossoms with a lavender umbrella to match. She wore a large red hat trimmed with gold that went with her kimono. It delighted his sickly sister.

On a visit home from Japan, Lou asked me to see a Japanese movie with him, just like in our younger days. Hawaii is so ethnically diverse that you have all sorts of things to experience on these small islands. So I attended my first non-American movie. The snow looked cold; the purple, white, and gold kimonos were beautiful; and the love story was done in such a grand style. Lou enjoyed it. As for me, it was a brand-new experience. I was so glad that there were English subtitles. Lou seemed to understand what the actors and actresses were saying. I was just trying to read fast enough to comprehend what was going on and take in the culture of Japan on the movie screen as well. Some of the cultural aspects were so interesting that I lost track of the subtitles and the plot and had to try to catch up throughout the movie. Lou sensed this.

After the movie, we went to eat at a Japanese restaurant at his insistence. "Okay, John, you've got to try this soup. Pretend that you are in Japan right now. Dig in, brah!" It was easy to do since we had just viewed a movie that was made in Japan. After slurping my first spoonful of soup, I made an amusing expression, at which he chuckled.

"You're trying to be funny, brother!" I blurted out. He had just finished his last traces of laughter, and he continued eating. The hot miso soup was laced with green onions and small cubes of white tofu. It was served along with salted cabbage, rice, fish, and other condiments. Our Asian meal tasted somewhat foreign to me, whereas he simply enjoyed it. One could clearly tell Japan was already part of him.

Chapter 3

What Is War Like?

The Vietnam War broke out in 1964 and continued until 1975. Lou reenlisted in the army in 1965 and stayed in the army until 1974. Who really understands why he did so? He fought in combat for five years and spent the rest as a combat medic. On every R & R Lou had, he always returned home to spend time with his family and me. During his stay, a whole string of tall bottles of whiskey, vodka, gin, and wine got emptied each night. He had never drank as much as now; perhaps this was an inception of another change in his life.

During this time, I had left my college studies for a while to get married and care for my parents, so I had picked up a part-time job as a hospital orderly. This allowed me to do what was needed and yet have funds coming in to pay the bills. It also allowed me to have some passing time with Lou whenever he came home.

On one occasion, he consumed so much alcohol that on the way to the kitchen, he swooned backward as he reached the sink and passed out cold on the wooden kitchen floor. I heard the heavy thud from another room and ran into the white-walled kitchen. There was Lou, lying straight out, cold, on the floor with his arms stretched out along his sides. When he came to, he asked, "Hey, what happened? Why am I on the floor?"

"Brother, you just passed out! You went down, just like that," I exclaimed. "You drank too much."

And he would simply say, "Never mind, I'm okay. I'm fine; don't worry," as his mother and I helped him up from the floor, with all three of us swaying while almost falling over one another. And again, everyone blamed the alcohol and not the drinker—the alcoholic—for his state of stupor. It was tradition, culture. It was all right.

During the inception of the war, Lou would spend time with me and share the atrocities that he had witnessed: the splattered blood of decapitated bodies, the slaughtering of the innocents, the body parts of his friends and other American soldiers hanging from the branches of trees, and the hardships that all people endured. He could not forget when, in 1966, a chopper had gone down and burned. "John, all the passengers and crew, sixteen in all, were piled up in front of the chopper." It was the first mass casualty that he had experienced, and he had to pull them out and bag the bodies. It hit him hard as he expressed to me, "Brah, I had just given the crew's chief some hand cream that very morning, and now here, now at night, I was pulling him and others who I knew out of the downed chopper! Damn!"

The awakenings of life continued to manifest. He witnessed two assault choppers flying too close to each other. In no time at all, their blades met, and he stood in horror as he saw both choppers fall end over end with the crew members still strapped inside. "John, now I know how my mother felt when she witnessed the sailor on the motorcycle climb the pole and drop down to the ground when Pearl Harbor was attacked on December 7, 1941."

Evidently, many veterans carry such memories with them. But these memories that are difficult to shake are carried along with feelings of shock, anger, compassion, aimlessness, and helplessness, all compacted into one solid mass. Maybe unknowingly at first, as time goes on, this compacted glob begins to seat itself comfortably in one's mind and body, becoming difficult to release.

While he conducted a class as a combat medic in 1968, a large explosion occurred nearby. Lou related how people started to yell, "Medic, medic, help, mess hall!"

"John, we just dropped everything in class and started to race toward the yelling that was increasing like thunder! As we approached the area, we were startled to see the ground covered with the wounded, bleeding and moaning in pain. I had to calm my men in order to have them concentrate on checking the wounded. It was so bad that I requested a flight surgeon as well." Using every split second wisely to save lives was of utmost importance. And this left Lou exhausted. He learned what sheer exhaustion meant. But did he know how to deal with what would come later, post-traumatic stress?

Shoving to the back of his mind the thunderous blasts and smoke from the bombings; the ongoing shots of fiery gunfire; the splattering of bright red blood; and the endless abuse to people, some of whom were totally innocent, Lou gradually saw what he could do to dull ongoing thoughts of these war experiences. This he did in a social manner. A group of soldiers and others decided to do a project to help the people there and, of course, add to their recreation. "John, we've built and refurbished a shack into a bar. We painted it red inside, painted the furnishings red, and we're even having red curtains made," he remarked with much humor. "And the bar is a hit, with the music swaying everyone and the drinks pouring to help wipe the horrors of war away. Wish you could see this, John," he said enthusiastically. They were so proud of their ability to renovate a structure that would entertain others and ease the atrocities experienced during their wartime service. During this time, Lou's drinking increased.

From July 1968 to February 1969, Agent Orange met Lou, his fellow comrades, and many other troops in an operation between the Hue and A Shau Valleys. Lou was with the 3rd Brigade, 187th Infantry Regiment, of the 101st Airborne Division. Agent Orange was sprayed a number of times a week in that mountainous jungle, and it affected everyone, including Lou. "John, we are covered with water blisters, skin rashes, and boils every time we go out to fight. At least we have the help of field medics, although we need medical care from doctors. We are not considered top priority if we are sent back to camp for real medical care, as there are the wounded and dead they have to attend to. Our commander colonel is very, very concerned." It got so bad that they were moved to a beach area to be free of the chemical burns on their bodies. These blisters would reappear throughout Lou's lifetime. Eventually, the water would turn into blood. One of the end results would be kidney cancer.

Soon after that, Lou phoned Ralph. "Dad, I want to build a church for these people. Can you help us? We need lumber." His dad replied that it would be difficult to ship lumber all the way to Vietnam. With a heavy heart, Lou's dad hung up the phone, wishing that he could help in another way.

On hearing this, I simply smiled and thought, *Hmm, that Lou! He really is all heart! From a bar to a church, he is seeing the importance of faith.*

***

"What, Angela Davis, the Black Panther organization!" Ralph yelled out as my heavy boot steps approached the kitchen door of their home. I was doing my weekly so-called family visit. "John, Lou just called. He is interested in the Black Panther organization. He feels that this war is unnecessary. John, talk sense to him. He has a war to fight and doesn't need to be involved in things that will bring about governmental scrutiny," Ralph pleaded as he handed the phone to me.

In a casual manner, I asked, "Hey, brother, what are you getting yourself into?"

"John, I know that Angela Davis is connected to communism, with which my folks do not agree. But she really is a great person. I met her and believe in some of what she is saying. And if communism takes care of their people—gives them jobs, a place to live—what is wrong with that part of communism? I just don't believe in the rest of it."

This was a time when many protests were being made against America's involvement in the Vietnam War. In the early '70s, pictures of student protesters who were shot at Kent University in Ohio by the National Guard covered the front page of newspapers throughout the States. Protests by individuals and groups ran rampage across the nation as well as throughout the world. Lou had to deal with this stage of protests in warfare on top of everything else. Other soldiers went through this also—some silently, others aggressively.

After our phone call, Lou just paid attention to the war. But he still had a deep respect for Angela Davis. Was it really that he thought the war was unnecessary, or was it that he disagreed with the politics involved at the expense of the soldiers?

Three months after our last phone call, I had a stroke, and life turned completely upside down. I could no longer hold on to my part-time job, let alone care for my parents. Other family members stepped in to care for them while my wife and I did the best we could with my disability. I was grateful, though, for the fact that I could still think, walk, talk, drive, and love people. As such, I could move along yet in life.

When Lou came home for an R & R, he sought to share the happiness of life that he knew with others to sort of perk me up. After visiting his aunt, who lived close by, he took his two brothers and sister to a popular nightclub, enjoying the drinking and dancing to lively music until the wee hours of the morning. He called my wife and me to join them, and we all had a great time. Enjoying time with his family meant much to him, and to me as well. In addition, it helped bolster his spirit for his return to war.

Four months later, he called and, as usual, after speaking to his parents, asked for me. Ralph and Lana shouted out the window, "John, hurry, come on over! Lou's on the phone and wants to speak to you."

As I hurried over to his home, I could feel his excitement over the phone. "Hey, brah, you know something, I'm a doc now," he exclaimed ecstatically over the phone.

"What do you mean, Lou? You're a doc?"

"Well, I delivered two babies! Boy, what an experience," he exclaimed as if riding on cloud nine. I could still feel the excitement lingering. "Yep, two babies. Now I realize what women go through in giving birth. John, I love being a medic! When these babies were delivered, when they came out into the world, what a wonderful feeling! And I assisted the mothers in their healing."

"Wow, Lou, just wonderful!" I responded to his excitement.

"Say, brah, I also ride the helicopters to rush in and pick up the wounded and …" he said, pausing with sadness, "the dead. They call me Doc. Imagine that—Doc!" he shouted while regaining himself over the phone.

And with that, he continued to help his fellow soldiers throughout the war. As a medic, he shared with me how he tended to all responsibilities that came with this job. He described cases dealing with trauma, changing soiled and bloody bandages, cleaning bullet wounds, dealing with blown-off body pieces and broken limbs, suturing, handling the wounded, even knowing that in some cases, no matter what you did, death was inevitable. "Brother John, this is a most wrenching experience: to know that they will die, and they look to you for hope till their last breath. It just tears at my heart." But he would not give up. He continued as a medic, coming under fire in the air and on the ground more than fifty times. The life of each individual soldier was too important to him. He witnessed the sacrifices that his fellow soldiers made for their country. Every life was too precious to lose. And he would tend to the wounded, defying death, until the Good Lord called the soul to God.

In one of my letters to Lou, I asked him what war was like. It was a rude awakening for me. He responded with such fury and rage. "War! What is war like! Don't ever ask that f---ing shit question, John. Ever!" That was how he began and how he ended his letter.

When I saw him again on R & R, he took the time to answer my question face-to-face. "John, you asked me in your last letter what war is like. I was really pissed at you when I read your letter. It took time for me to realize that you really didn't understand and knew shit about war except for what you read in newspapers and see on the news channels. John, war is putting yourself in danger for God, your family, and your country. And more! The real reason for my fighting this war is for freedom—the freedom for all the children in our nation, in every single state of America, to walk this earth freely. Brah, I fight so that they will be able to go out and see a movie whenever they want to, to walk the streets at any time during the day or night, to play in the river and enjoy its fish and crystal-clear water, and to play at the park with their friends."

"Wait, Lou," I said, "I didn't mean to offend you at all. I was just curious to hear from someone who really knows—you know, someone who is in the war, having firsthand experiences, and knows what he's talking about. So why not ask you, my brother?"

He nodded and continued. "War is also about seeing the ugliness of humankind, such as seeing the body parts of your comrades hanging from the branches of trees—their ears, noses, fingers, arms, and legs. The enemy did this, and that's not the worst of it. Their private parts were cut off, their dicks and balls stuffed into their mouths or ears. Man, they were my buddies. And to see them like that! You know what it does to you? Shock, anger, anger!" he shouted. "And then the fear starts, and you experience what it means to be scared. It's enough to make you go nuts! I tell you, John, it is a psychological war! You witness innocent people being killed, and sometimes, you are placed in that situation and have no other choice. You see soldiers unraveling while you can only stand by helplessly. So much tears you apart psychologically and physically." He then revealed to me how the blistering on his side was turning red from direct exposure to Agent Orange.

And I thought, *What an opportune time to tell Lou of my encounter with a spirit that terrified me so horrendously that I could have died of fright.* Although it could not be seen, its sounds and heavy breathing were so frightening that I just froze as it approached me, coming nearer and nearer to where I was sitting. Fear overtook my entire being as it stood close to me, heaving. I could not call out for help even though another person was in the room with me. With all my soul's strength, I called upon the Holy Name of Jesus, and it immediately left. It was my being against another being, my spirit against another spirit, my soul against another soul. It was a most fearsome experience. What to do? Have faith. I deeply understood what Saint John of the Cross meant years later when I read his writings as advised by a holy one.

But before I had a chance to share this with Lou, the bottles of whiskey, vodka, and gin performed their disappearing act before midnight in their clear glass costumes.

Chapter 4

Sleeping with the Dead: Revelations

On another R & R, Lou said, "John, I even slept with three corpses of the Viet Cong Army in my tent, each one piled on top of another. The bodies had to be kept in my tent until an investigation was done. There was nowhere else to put them. I couldn't take it! The stench from the body fluids seeping out so freely—damn, the smell of death was unbearable! So dreadful! Do you know what it's like to sleep alongside dead bodies, even if they are covered? It's dreadful!" he screamed.

I felt like discussing eschatology with him at this point, including my experiences of the afterlife. I wanted to tell him that these souls were alive in the spirit world, having traveled through the dark tunnel toward the light at the end, just as I had done. If only I could share with him that their thoughts took on a spiritual reality without having to travel through time, over distance, or in space, as I had experienced.

In the flash of a thought, I was in my friend's house on another island at 5:00 a.m. I heard his daughter enter the house and call out to him and listened to his reply. But then I knew that I had to return to my body. I had an awareness that I was on my bed, where I had gone to sleep. In an instant, I went back through the light and black tunnel. When I awoke in my body, I called my friend and told him that his daughter had visited him at 5:00 a.m., and I relayed the greetings and conversation that they had shared.

He responded, "That is true, John! How do you know this?"

I explained to him the experience granted to me. Suddenly, all my learnings about life after our physical death came to full enlightenment. There is no end to life. Was God teaching me something? Then I realized what Ralph went through when he had tended to the dead bodies in makeshift tents at Pearl Harbor.

Lou continued to express the sufferings he was experiencing. I had to let him get his fears and frustrations out of his system. So I just continued to listen without interrupting.

"The Viet Cong knew what to do to strain us, anything to make us deranged and crazy!" he shouted. "They would use us against ourselves. So damn cunning and very insidious. We Americans had to do things that would be hard on us."

Then I began to understand why he detested my question "What is war like?" A lesson well learned.

"John, they would even send children into our camp areas, knowing that many of our men have families and children. They also knew that we would give the children chocolate candy bars just because they were children, and this would be a most gratifying and delightful treat for them, especially being exposed to all the sufferings found in the war. Hell, we loved candies as kids too. Still do." Then he paused. "Well, the children just wanted the candy! And we had compassion for them. John, the Viet Cong were using the children as their spies. When they would enter our areas, they would look around and report back to the Viet Cong. After the children would leave, later on at night, we would be attacked. And the enemy knew exactly where to go to do the most damage. They knew!" he cried out angrily.

"Children are exploited throughout the entire world, not only in the slave trade, in jobs, and in divorces but even in war. Sometimes, these children would get found out and would have to be shot to death to prevent more of our soldiers from being killed. It had to be done. The evil of war!" The chorus line of shots of whiskey followed, one after another, in endless succession.

Then he continued to an often-repeated event, time and time again, especially when on his last bottles of booze. "There was My Lai! My Lai, My Lai! We just killed them, all the men, women, and children. For no reason—no damn reason at all," he would slur with tears running down his face contorted in psychological pain, thus revealing the suffering deep within his soul. Evidently, this bothered Lou deeply. Another Trail of Tears. Within an hour and a half, another bottle of whiskey or vodka would do its dance and then disappear. Lou was the only one drinking.

Whenever Lou got a grip on himself, he would then slur the same stories or events over and over again. "Yeah, Charlie [Viet Cong] sent kids into our camps. Typical Americans that we are, we gave them candy bars, because we know that kids love candy, especially chocolate candy. But they sent them to snitch on us. Shit! Those bastards!" And he would fall asleep murmuring, "My Lai … A Shau Valley, A Shau Valley."

With all the atrocities of war, such as at My Lai, I began to wonder about the perspective the Vietnamese, the Viet Cong, had of us Americans. Was it as ugly as ours regarding what was done to our soldiers? Perhaps it was more so for the Vietnamese people, since the war was on their soil. Hatred, anger to the point of spiritual curses? But maybe asking for forgiveness had already come to a close as time had traveled and they had found understanding and peace.

When Lou found out later that one of his nieces was on phenobarbital and then Dilantin due to seizures, he remarked, "Gee, that's what the children are given in Vietnam to help them deal with the bombings and their fear of war. We use it to help the children keep calm during the bombings. You know, John, they just shiver as the loud explosions run across their pathways. They're damn scared, and they just run anywhere or freeze in their tracks. It's hard to see the fear and feel the trembling of the innocent ones. War is hell for everyone. And yet it is for freedom," he would say with much frustration in his voice. It was clear how Lou thought of the children in wartime, at the same time revealing his commitment to fighting the war.

And that is how it went during the war years: sharing, celebrating, being afraid, and conversing on his visits home as if time was running out. And it was. He would be gone, back to war, in no time at all. The empty bottles of hard booze—whiskey, vodka, and gin—would be left behind, sitting on the kitchen counter or floor, laced with memories of combat and destruction. Standing tall alongside, as if on watch, were empty bottles of beer, a substitute for whiskey, vodka, gin, or rum, when nothing else was available to cope with his life.

On one visit home, Lou wanted to go to a bar for a drink but didn't want to go alone. So he decided to take one of his nephews with him. "John, you should have seen the girls fall all over my nephew!" he told me. "'Oh, he's so cute!' they all said. Man, I had so much attention from them."

"Lou, what are you doing, taking your nephew with you, to a bar? He's only four years old!"

"Brah, that's how I get the girls to come by me!" he said with a smile while chuckling.

The very next day, as I was working in a second-floor printer's office, a car drove by close to the building. *Beep, beep. Beep, beep,* sounded the car horn. With curiosity, I went to the window and peered down below. There was Lou in his green army fatigues, sitting behind the wheel of a black dune buggy with his four-year-old nephew in a light blue T-shirt and jeans with an army helmet on his head, sitting alongside him. Both were laughing and having a grand time!

"Hey, John, we just came from a bar. We had a good time!" he shouted up to the window where I was standing. After an exchange of words, off they went, in the roaring black dune buggy, both chuckling, the soldier and his four-year-old bar buddy. This was four in the afternoon.

"Well, you know, brah, how some of us single guys need our social life, even during wartime," he related gleefully as he began another R & R. "So early one morning, here I was, coming back through the jungle of trees and bushes to base after a nice night's stay with this pretty lady, and when I reached a pit, Charlie surrounded me. They came out of nowhere. Man, I thought I was a goner. I was so scared, scared shitless, thinking, *This is it. I'm gonna die!* Man, I found God so fast. Now wait, maybe just for a moment. And, brah, when the bullets were flying all around me, this black guy, James, who was just coming around the bend of a mountain on a narrow path above, heard the shooting. He looked down and saw me in the shallow ditch at the mercy of Charlie, surrounded with only green shrubbery to protect me, nowhere to run. I was completely circled and hemmed in like a caged animal. James, without a second thought, opened fire. And I'm here today," he calmly remarked as he closed his eyes for a few seconds. A moment of thankfulness.

"You know something, John? I never did like blacks before, and I don't know why. I did not have the healthy attitude like some of the folks from the plantation days who loved and accepted everyone and called ethnic groups nicknames only for fun, not out of cruelty. I was blinded by the prejudice of others and called them derogatory words because others did. But after this happened, my mind was flung open, and I thought, *Where the hell have I been?* I really respect them, especially my new friend, Jimmy. I didn't know him before he came to help me. Funny how life's experiences make us see things in reality. Boy, how blinded I was by the generations of racism that were perpetuated in America and abroad."

"Well, at least one good thing came out of this war!"

"John, shut the f--- up!"

I couldn't help but grin and interject, "Lou, many of us grow up blinded by prejudice and racism for no reason at all. This cultural blindness carries on for generation after generation until it becomes like a bad habit. Unfortunately, some people refuse to see the reality of life and live it, and prejudice becomes a self-fulfilling prophecy. Slavery, Hitler, and the KKK are prime examples of the harassing and killing of ethnic groups, all for power, greed, and land, hidden behind the erroneous and false facade of God's name. It stems from satanic pride, that which sets out to blaspheme the Holy Spirit. Look at the blindness regarding Jesus Christ. Did He not have a mixed background? Look at the three wise men: African, Asian, and cosmopolitan. Was not coconut oil given? Food for thought, my friend, food for thought! Centuries of prejudice also surrounded Jesus."

"You mean Jesus had olive skin?" he asked with his eyebrows lifted with wonderment.

"I guess you could say that. Shucks, Lou, look at some other blind spots in the Bible that are somewhat related to a form of prejudice. Now, you may disagree with me on this, but it seems kind of odd, don't you think? Abraham being told to have relations with a slave girl? Sounds more like a human decision, not a divine one. Could that not be an excuse for cultural pride? It is no wonder that a love triangle developed. Unfortunately, you know how that goes. Some may say that to cover up, they shoved the slave girl out with her son. Others say that they were allowed to remain. Whatever version was accepted, for hundreds of years, Christians bowed down to it because somebody wrote that God said so! Brother, God is not mean. So I got to thinking, was the offering by Abraham of his son, Isaac, to God an act of atonement or just out of love for God?"

"What are you saying, brah?"

"Just thinking out of the box. Am I glad God finally got everybody squared away, including Abraham? He might be a saint today. Who knows."

***

On his next visit home, Lou appeared calmer than usual. We sat sipping our drinks on the porch of his home in the shade with a nice breeze passing by. "Now, John," he began, "what's that crazy talk that we had on my last visit on blind spots? Did you—"

"Another blind spot, Lou? Yeah, there seems to be some that are of particular interest to me, such as the holy mother, the mother of Jesus."

"Okay, okay, what about the mother of Jesus?"

"It is written in the Holy Bible, Paul's letter to the Ephesians, 5:31–33, that in marriage, the two will become as one. If she is the spouse of the Holy Spirit, then she is one with the Holy Spirit! Paul goes on further to express that 'there is a deep secret truth revealed in this scripture ... applying to Christ and the church.'"

Looking at me with an enigmatic expression, he squirted out, "Yeah, so what ... What the hell? What goes ... what is it that Christians say, something about three in one? You know, that geometric shape—yeah, yeah, the triangle!"

"Hey, brother, check out John's gospel and his letters. The other gospels also talk about it in an esoteric way, but Saint John says over and over again that the Son is one with the Father. So now, if that is so, that the Son is one with the Father, the heart of the Trinity depicts the Father, Son, and Holy Spirit as one. And because the mother is one with the Holy Spirit as spouse, the heart of the Trinity depicts God as love.

"Here is one way to view it, Lou. Jesus was the visible image of the Father given to humankind. And in order for the Holy Spirit, one with the Father, to manifest Itself, Jesus had to come in the flesh through Mary, His mother, who, as spouse of the Holy Spirit, is one in union with the Holy Spirit. When the Word became flesh, the mother raised Him under the guidance of the Holy Spirit. The Holy Spirit not only manifested itself at Christ's baptism through the voice of the Father in the River Jordan but also through the teaching of Jesus's ministry and came in fullness after the resurrection of Jesus. Our Heavenly Father speaks directly through the Holy Spirit and is seen and also heard through the Son."

"What was that, John? Huh?" he inquired, seemingly lost in thought.

"Brother, through the Holy Spirit, the mother bears the Word, meaning that the Son came in the flesh and the inception of the church was therefore established on earth and in heaven. Could the hidden secret lie here, or something to that effect? This immense love is for us. Don't forget, Lou; read John's first epistle, all of chapters 4 and 5. Maybe this accounts for the Son's ascension—rising on His own into heaven, body and soul—and the mother being assumed—raised into heaven, body and soul."

"Hey, John, wait a minute, wait! Are you okay, brah? Are you feeling okay? You always go off on a tangent. Always thinking way out of the box! Get back here. Remember back on one of my visits, we were talking about prejudices in our lives, and that was how these blind spots came about? Didn't you also have some prejudice against the blacks?"

"Not much, Lou. But that's because we were brainwashed. Maybe it is because people were afraid to understand them over a century ago. They might have come to the conclusion that blacks are equal to whites but were afraid to admit it. That is real satanic pride. It's the same as how women are portrayed in the Bible."

"Oh no, there he goes again. Oh shit!"

"Look, friend, because of Jewish tradition and maybe cultural pride among other ethnic groups during the time of Christ, women were looked upon as being of not much importance. Jesus showed them the opposite. Jesus met them at the well and spoke with them, showing how they are as deserving of respect as men. Because of this past cultural perspective, which may be different today, I think we lost a lot of information on the mother of Jesus. But that is what cultural pride does in every ethnic group on earth. Sometimes, it blinds the mind to truths if we do not use common sense."

"Well, at least we know that Mary is the mother of Jesus."

"I guess so, brother, but wait; let me think. Now, you don't have to agree with me," I stated with a pause.

"Knock it off, John; just share with me, at least. And by the way, are you that interested in whether I agree with you or not?"

"Not really. Just listening to me is good enough! Now, Lou, think of it. Who took care of Jesus from the time He was born, knowing that He was given to her only to be crucified to open hell to release us? Did she not know her role as the mother of God as events were unfolding? As Luke states in 2:14–19, 'Mary pondered over what was said and kept things in Her Heart.' Who taught, guided, and prepared Him to accomplish the will of God the Father? And He reminded her when He was found after He went missing following the Passover feast. 'Did you not know that I have to be about my Father's business?' His mother and Joseph understood Him—Joseph, the pinnacle of support to the mother and the Son.

Lou, do you remember hearing about a wedding feast at Cana and how the host ran out of wine for his guests?"

"Brah, you're going off on another tangent. But yeah, I remember hearing something about it. Also, Jesus was not going to do anything about it until His mother pointed it out. And He just performed the miracle of changing water into wine without hesitation. Wow!"

"Well, don't you think Jesus knew His mother well? She didn't have to beg Him to do so. She just pointed it out. And even when Jesus related to her that it was not His time yet, she simply told the servants to do whatever He said. And boom! It was done. You know what, Lou? Jesus knew the authority of His mother—John 2:1–11."

"Wow, awesome, John!"

"Besides, who stood on the sidelines with sorrow beyond human understanding as He carried His cross and fell three times? And who stood at the foot of His cross to give Him the last bit of courage to complete His mission? Lou, face it. What woman would bear such immense pain for all of humanity in her Divine Son, our Lord, who was going through it Himself, paying the price for each one of us? And yet, as she stood with the essence of pain going through her entire being, not a word did she speak even as her Son gave up His Spirit. She simply cried in utter silence for the abashment and pain of what her Son had to endure for all of humanity while also shouting in spiritual joy, for souls would now be released from the bondage of hell through her Divine Son."

"Hey, John, what about—"

"Another point to consider, Lou: wasn't it told to Mary that a sword shall pierce the heart of her soul?—Luke 2:34. Look at those two symbols, brother: a sword and a cross. I have seen drawings of the Sacred Heart of Jesus with a crown of thorns around it, with drops of blood falling from a gash in its side, and a cross on top of the heart enveloped in flames of love for us. This really depicts the love of the Son for us and the Father's purpose for His coming in the flesh. And there was also a heart for Mary, pierced with a sword, with a garland of flowers and flames of love at the top. I think a dove should have been there in the flames since she is the spouse of the Holy Spirit. Anyway, from what is written, she is one with the Holy Spirit."

"Enough, John! Hey, man, stop this shit for a moment. No wonder we have a mixed-up nation! Get, get, and get back to my thoughts."

"Oh, okay, okay. Sorry, Lou; just had to share some thoughts with you. You don't have to agree with me. You know that."

"Well, now that we are back on my trend of thought, tell me, John, what you can say about the color black that would undo the brainwashing of our young years."

"Let me begin, Lou, in this way. Black is the ultimate beauty of the mixture of all the colors of the rainbow. It lets you know that you are not alone when you see your shadow. Lou, you always will have company."

"Yeah, brah, I get one big shadow with this body of mine. Ha!"

"It has warmth, for it absorbs and does not reflect light; it provides coolness in the shade of a tree; it is rich in nature, for it gives depth to all that exists and, as a result, accentuates and gives splendor to all in creation; it provides the clarity of printed words that do not strain the eyes as other colors do. Black complements white as white complements black; both exist within and without, in harmony and distinction, neither being better than the other. Human beings must learn from the colors."

"Okay, okay, that's enough. I believe you."

"Got to go now, Lou. See you later."

He heaved a heavy sigh of relief and leaned back in his chair as if to say, *Go, and get the hell out of here. Peace at last,* and, *My God, what is happening to my friend?*

We continued our conversations later on another visit home. This time, Lou spent days at my house on his R & R. I saw something eating him up inside, and he just came out with it. "John, it is agonizing, with what I am doing in the war." I asked him what he meant by that statement.

"It agonizes me when I deal with so many of the injured and dying soldiers, the countless dead, and especially those on the brink of death. Yeah, that's the hardest," he said mournfully. "John, you and I know that life is precious. We have got to think of the life of every single soldier. You just don't know until you deal with it all." I could see a heart heavily laden with sorrow. He loved his fellow comrades in war. And the bottles of hard liquor did their disappearing act until sleep took over or when he just passed out.

One night, Lou just let it out. "John, the most devastating battle that I had difficulty accepting in the Vietnam War was the battle at Hamburger Hill in 1969. Man, some of our troops were just out of high school. They were our young boys—eighteen and nineteen years old, some twenty or twenty-one—who were just beginning life. And there, at A Shau Valley, they were to take the hill." He agonized, continuously moving his head from left to right. "A large number of the older soldiers knew that it might be total slaughter. And yet it had to be done," he whispered tearfully. "Yep, it had to be done. They are our true heroes!"

About ten minutes went by as Lou continued to mourn his young troops. Then, when he regained his composure, I decided to continue the conversation. "Lou, that was the same with Judas Iscariot."

"What the hell does Judas have to do with Hamburger Hill, John? I'm talking about how only young boys were sent up that damn hill! And you are giving me shit about Judas!"

"Oops. Well, I agree with you in that it could—could or should have been fought with more experienced soldiers and not those straight out of high school, and with better warfare equipment and supplies and correct strategic maneuvers so as not to kill our own soldiers. *Friendly fire*, I believe it is called. There was a choice here, I think." I felt that I had put my foot in my mouth as words kept stumbling out of it. What a fatuitous blunder on my part! "But the point I am making is that sometimes things have to be done. It is the same with Jesus; it had to be done a certain way. Jesus had to be betrayed."

"What, no, He didn't!" Lou shouted. "Brah, it was that damn evil guy's fault—that greedy Judas guy."

"Wait, Lou, wait! Jesus Christ kept saying over and over that it was the will of God the Father that He suffers, be put to death, and rise on the third day. Ultimately, Jesus was to destroy the gates of hell so that we all can be taken up to the Lord if we are deserving of such. Brother, it is found in Holy Scripture many times over. In Matthew's gospel, it is mentioned more than four times, in Mark's gospel more than six times, in Luke more than four times, and in John more than six times. Even when Peter tried to say the opposite—that it would not happen, the normal thinking of the average human—Jesus rebuked the devil out of the way from Peter. You can find this in Matthew's and Mark's gospels when Jesus says in response to Peter, 'Get behind me, Satan, because you think not God's thoughts but those of men.'"

"So where the hell does this so-called Judas fit in?" asked Lou in an impatient manner, stomping his right foot on the floor, muttering under his breath, "That f--- Judas over my young troops, no way!"

"Brother, the crucifixion of Jesus Christ had to be done to open the gates of hell. It was the Father's will. It was the most misunderstood plan of salvation for all of humankind for hundreds of years, except for those whom the Father wanted to reveal it to. Many could not equate this with love on the human level, so Jesus the Christ had to give Judas the courage to carry out the Father's divine will at the Last Supper. From all the gospel accounts, it appears that the apostles did not look forward to this. They even changed the subject as to who was the greatest among them, a topic that seemed to interest them, at least more than once."

"Who would, John? Imagine giving up your best friend to death."

"Yes, Lou, but remember, Christ kept saying over and over again that it was the Father's will. They heard it repeatedly over time. Perhaps Judas was the only one who knew the severity of it. And when he was told that he was the betrayer, before fear could take over Judas, the Holy Spirit intervened with the words of Jesus: 'Go quickly, and do what you must!' Jesus Christ knew that Judas was weakening and needed support to carry out our Heavenly Father's divine will. I find John's gospel to be the most updated, probably because it may have been the last written. Anyway, Lou, immediately after Judas left, Jesus Christ stated, 'Now the Son of man is glorified, and God is glorified in connection with him. And God will himself glorify him, and he will glorify him immediately.' The will of God the Father was finally being carried out. The role of Judas … ah."

"Hey, brah, this is kind of puzzling to me. I have to read the Bible to understand what you are trying to say." Lou had regained his composure.

"Lou, check this out. In John's gospel, even the soldiers hesitated to arrest Jesus. Judas was most probably feeling scared and guilty and hating himself already then and there. But Jesus said, 'Of those whom you have given me, I have not lost a single one.' At this point, Judas was still in good graces with the Lord. Unfortunately, the question remains as to what happened to Judas after this. Most probably Judas accompanied Peter to the sentencing of Jesus since he did know the high priests after turning Him over to them. Like Peter, who wept bitterly after denying Jesus three times, after witnessing the sentencing of Jesus, Judas may have given into greed earlier, but as Matthew moves us to see the real Judas, Judas, too, felt remorse and threw the thirty pieces of silver back into the temple. It states that the money was used for a potter's field to bury strangers. This is also stated in the Acts of the Apostles, fulfilling Jeremiah's former and David's latter prophecy. I do wonder about remorse, though. Don't you think that when people feel remorse, as opposed to despair, they want to make amends or make up for it? And Judas did by returning the pieces of silver."

"Yeah, but John, I think that when remorse turns to despondency, or when a person is in a state of severe despair, the lack of support along with unheeded cries for help, whether audible or not, could easily turn one's perspective, damn, into suicide."

"Brother Lou, now that is a real hell, suicide, because once you are on the other side, you can't settle the problems on earth, where you exited from. You hope that someone could help settle it. That is why prayers are so important. We need to ask God to guide the soul to the eternal light of Jesus."

"Sometimes that is so, John. Sometimes death is the fastest way out, or depending on the person's outlook, it could be the noblest thing to do. Shit, look at the Japanese kamikaze pilots during World War II. They committed suicidal attacks with their planes on large ships. Hey, giving up one's life according to one's cultural perspective and belief was considered extremely noble. Brah, this is the same for the terrorist human bombs of today in Iran. Wonder if brainwashing could be involved in any way? You know, like commitment versus brainwashing."

"Well, you know, brother, Saint Matthew further states that Judas hanged himself. Maybe so, or was he murdered by those who hated him for guiding the soldiers to Jesus to have Him arrested? Boy, he must have been hated and despised by many of Christ's followers who did not understand the importance of his role in fulfilling the divine plan of the Holy Trinity, a role that even Judas himself feared somewhat. This was certainly no form of brainwashing, for there is too much evidence in Christ's life to conclude otherwise."

"Or, brah, did Judas commit hara-kiri?" Lou interjected just as he finished reading Acts of the Apostles 1:16–20 from a Bible that I had just given him to read. "If it was for amends, and his intestines fell out, then that could be it. You see, John, hara-kiri or seppuku was done by the samurais or others that wanted to make up for shame or dishonor or for loyalty to a master that was dead." Thus spoke the scholarly military veteran as I sat there in a state of shock, listening to him.

Then I got hold of myself. "I would think that hara-kiri would fit Judas, Lou, because he was loyal to Jesus, his Master, to the end. But now, isn't that against the fifth commandment? Ultimately, life belongs to God, and whenever we accomplish our mission on earth, we are taken to His heavenly kingdom. If we leave this earth otherwise, again, this is where prayers are needed. I really don't know how God handles this, but doesn't that make sense? Yet, on the other hand, God can just do things regardless of if it makes sense to us or not."

"Brah, you're losing me now. Come on; get back on track."

"Anyway, Lou, when Jesus died, there were only different levels of hell."

"Wait, John, what about the other places that I heard churches speak about—purgatory and limbo?"

"Brother, I think, now, you don't have to agree with me, but maybe … purgatory is where the souls are working their way up to God. You know, like going through different levels or degrees. It appears as how we grow on earth, how we get to know God and want to move toward His Kingdom. And limbo seems to be a place where all the good souls wait for Jesus to come and free them from hell. In John's gospel, 5:25–30, Jesus predicts what will happen with His death: that the dead will hear the voice of the Son of God, that all souls who did good things will resurrect, and that those who lived a vile life will be subject to judgment. Thus, by His death, He unchained the gates of hell, and all the saints arose: Matthew 27:52, the New Testament. This appears to be the first judgment. But now, all the vile souls, unless they repent and work their way to God, will be in the final judgment. Remember, our Lady of Fatima asked us to pray for the souls of sinners in hell."

"What in the hell, John? Aren't they supposed to be damned for eternity?"

"Lou, the mother of God asked us to pray for the souls of sinners in hell. There may be other explanations that we are unaware of, especially if oral tradition was given and passed down from generation to generation and not preserved in writings."

"So what? Unless a soul wants God, then he or she can move toward Him?"

"Maybe. Or with prayers, and the most powerful being the Mass, the soul of a sinner is given or able to see a glimmer of light, spiritually speaking, and has the freedom to make the choice. The choice is given. But will it be at the right level to make it over the threshold toward God? Prayers will move the soul forward toward God. If the soul of a sinner chooses not to and prefers to choose evil, then the soul—or demon— remains in death, seeking to destroy others for eternity until God ends it all. But guess what, Lou? What if the evil one—the devil—repents and chooses God to worship eternally? Look at all the foolish souls of sinners that chose evil as their eternity—demons! Wouldn't all of them be eliminated? Period."

"Shit, John, is this really how it is?"

"Maybe ... something like that. Maybe God will reveal more to others, or already has, to help us understand. Maybe we really don't have to understand and can just follow Jesus."

"Hey, brah, you really make me think, even though it may be out of the box and somewhat like funny thinking! Ha-ha."

"Anyway, guess what, Lou? Who do you think Jesus must have bumped into when He descended into hell? Someone who most probably asked for His forgiveness for giving in to greed and selling His robe for money. Whether he hanged himself to repay God as an act of atonement or was murdered or committed ... What's that word, Lou? The point is that he must have loved the Lord so very much knowing what he had to do to carry out the will of God the Father. But the negative side of this was that it would result in generation after generation hating and despising Judas to the point of condemning him to the eternal hell, not just a level of hell, and therefore, it would have been better that he not be born—Matthew 26:24 from the New Testament—and Judas knew this. Maybe this is where fear stepped in. Fear distorts the connection of our humanness to our spirituality. It became too much for Judas to bear to see his beloved Jesus suffer and be condemned to death because of His wanting to help carry out the Father's will. So his human side was weakened. Maybe.

"This outlook on Judas, being condemned to everlasting hell, has gone on century after century, even up to the year 2003 and beyond. Maybe, not so any longer, once the love of God is understood, and how forgiving God is. Brother, Judas must have went up into heaven with Jesus Christ, along with Abraham, Moses, David, and all other souls deserving of such. Hell, Lou, look at how these guys sinned. See how Peter denied the will of God the Father and also denied knowing Jesus due to fear and yet was put in charge of the Church. God truly understands our human limitations and struggles and is a very merciful God when we are truly sorry for our transgressions and we change our lives and make amends for the wrong that we have committed. Judas must be the greatest saint in heaven! Who knows?"

"John, where the hell do you come up with this kind of thinking? You are so eccentric! No, you are an eccentric!"

"Lou, you don't have to agree with me, but thanks for just listening. I'm just sharing what my friends and I discuss. Look at it this way, Lou. If God forgave Judas, who gave in to greed; forgave Moses, who almost lost faith—hell, forty years in the desert is too long for anyone—and forgave Abraham and David, and many others, even Mary Magdalene, shucks, Lou, we got a chance to get to heaven."

"Okay, John, no doubt, you are the Eccentric. You are one crazy bastard, you know!"

That night ended with the calmness of "Silent Night" and tittering over jokes. Bottles of liquor did their curtain call with great applause.

On a later R & R, we wasted no time and went deep into our conversation. "By the way, Lou, why did they call it Hamburger Hill?"

"Oh hell, John, that was because the Americans were shot into bloody shreds so their bodies looked like raw hamburger meat. My boys! They were my boys! My young men!" Tears flooded his eyes, and pain shadowed his face again, revealing the sorrow in his heart and the agony in his body. I had never seen Lou cry agonizingly, except when he gave up his son in divorce and whenever he recounted the loss of lives that had been in his reach. In some instances, he was given the right to save lives; in others, it was out of his control. Hamburger Hill just kept tearing him apart, and the alcohol would be consumed like an unstoppable gas pump. Serving four tours in the war was enough to push anyone over the edge. Or so I thought.

Breaking the silence, he blurted out, "So, John, what's new with you?"

"I'm looking for a spiritual director to help guide me spiritually."

"What was that? What did you say?"

He passed out cold on the soft settee before I could answer him the second time. I did wonder if he did that conveniently. After throwing a blanket over him, I lightly wiped his tears away.

On one of his R & R visits home in the early '70s, Lou decided to spend a couple of nights at my home again. The ritual of downing bottles of whiskey, vodka, gin, and whatever drinks replenished the cabinet began its usual chorus-line performance. I just sat and listened to his war experiences. Lou went on about leeches sucking on their skin as they crossed rivers during monsoon season. He laughed as he described how they used cigarettes to burn them off their skin. He made light of almost everything with his lighthearted chuckle. And he was able to move on.

Later that night, we decided to turn in. In the middle of the night, I was suddenly awakened by yelling from the living room. Lou was sleeping in his usual bed at my house, the settee in the parlor. "Charlie, Charlie!" Lou was shouting.

I got out of bed and ran from the bedroom to the living room. Lou was sitting up on the settee in the dark, soaking wet with body sweat. His arms were positioned as if holding a rifle and ready to shoot. I quickly turned the light on. "Lou, you okay?" I asked.

"Sorry, John, just had a nightmare," he muttered. "I'll be all right. I'm okay." He wanted to be alone. In seclusion.

I turned off the light and in the dark quietly went back to my bedroom, where my wife was still in a deep sleep as if there were no war going on. And I heard a faint whisper coming from the living room: "My Lai"— silence—"My Lai," followed by groaning.

It was during this time that Lou's second marriage failed in less than a year. About it, he said, in a melancholy tone, "I take full blame for it, John. I just can't keep anything good anymore. I don't know why. I don't know—just don't know. I think it's best that I never marry again. I have a hard time keeping my own life together. Something is wrong with me. I have so much anger that I become violent. And the nightmares! Drinking really helps me cope." The devastation of war attacked Lou's entire life and being.

***

In 1973, a cease fire was signed in Paris. But it was not until 1975 that the war fully came to an end.

In 1974, Lou called and told me that he was going to request a discharge. This flabbergasted me. With much excitement, I shouted at him, "Lou, you have only two more years to go, and then you can retire. Don't lose it all! What are you doing to your life? You already gave seventeen years in service of our country!"

In a serious tone, he responded, "John, I just can't take it anymore. I can't. I really can't. Something is wrong with me, and I don't know what it is."

"What do you mean, Lou? You came this far; don't throw it away. Think of your son."

"John, I also respect our efforts to fight for freedom, for our democracy. But brah, I don't agree with how the war is fought. I am about to be disciplined. I just couldn't agree anymore. You know something? We need to think of each individual soldier. We need to fight a war where we win. We should always have a military and political victory plan. Too many lives are lost, suffering. I just disagree at this point. But I agree to fight for America—democratic America."

Although I knew that Lou wanted so much to make the military his career, after serving in the Korean Conflict, going on four tours in Vietnam, and helping his fellow veterans, undoubtedly, the end was in sight. With just two more years to go until retirement, he just couldn't take it any longer. The atrocities of war took their toll. His drinking was way out of control, and he would go into extreme states of rage. I knew by the tone of his voice and his conviction and commitment to his fellow soldiers, dead or alive, that this was the end of his active career dedicated to them. But I was wrong in a sense.

Request for Discharge: February 27, 1974

America does not need an old army; our country needs a new army. It will not be generals or colonels or captains or sergeants that will make the new army, but instead, it will be the individual soldier. This soldier must be trained in military duties, but he must also be under constant political indoctrination. What is right is to constantly remind the troops of their country's history and the institutions that helped to make America a great nation. This is one way of rebuilding the young soldier's pride in his country and the army. I cite the ability of a little man in blue pajamas with a straw hat and an AK-47 to withstand the tactical strength, technology, and massive firepower of the US forces as a tribute to effective political training. Constant political indoctrination overcomes fear and strives to make one's country, a great nation.

I no longer wish to make the lives of my troops miserable. This feeling is motivated by the experience of seeing the individual soldier make so many sacrifices in combat. It was my honor and sorrow to pick up the American soldier when he was injured, wounded, or dead. His bravery will always live in my heart.

I respectfully request an honorable discharge under chapter 10, AR 635-200, based on my past record. This action is for the good of the service.

Signed,
Lou

Lou served in the Korean Conflict Era, in the Vietnam Era, and during peacetime. He entered as a combat soldier and left as a combat medic.

Chapter 5

The Monster Emerges:
PTSD, Alcoholism, and Anger

After being honorably discharged in May 1974, Lou found himself again at war. This time, the enemies were post-traumatic stress disorder (PTSD), alcoholism, Agent Orange, and anger, all rolled into one. This was the final war that Lou would fight for his fellow veterans, alcoholics, and chemical abusers. At first, he continued to fight this war with alcohol on a daily basis, a false weapon he picked up in his youth that he had used to its fullest in wartime as he grew older. Still dealing with the bright red blood blisters that bled on his left side, and the nightmares of war, Lou sought some compensation from the government he so faithfully served but to no avail. In fact, doctors did not believe him when he told them about how his torso would bleed.

Because of his love for music and singing in his younger years, when the war was over, Lou headed for the East Coast. No one heard from Lou for some time. He dropped out of sight. He simply didn't want to associate with people. He didn't know who to trust—this being an effect of PTSD. Then suddenly he would pop up from out of nowhere over the phone. Everyone was so concerned, asking him where in the world he had been all that time. He would simply respond that he had to tend to some things, saying, "I'm okay. Don't worry; I'm fine."

The following month, he called home and with excitement said, "John, you and my family have just got to come here. This is where the artists are—the writers, the singers! You have to see Greenwich Village. Man, it's so nice!" He went on to describe the open-air cafés, the colorful canopies of royal blue and mauve, the delicious smells of foods and freshly baked breads as you strolled along the sidewalks lined with green, leafy branches cascading from tree trunks. "There are even institutes for the arts, performing and filming. John, close by is Little Italy, and oh, you gotta taste them sausages." It was as if Lou was taking us on a tour of Manhattan.

During his next call home, he stated, "Hey, John, there is a great university here, in Uptown Manhattan, called Columbia University. Try to convince my brothers to come to this university. It would be good for them. There is a good education program here." And he continued on, talking about the Horace Mann Building and other buildings and museums, Harlem, and the greenery of trees and shrubbery and the lakes in Central Park. But most important to him was the Juilliard School's Music Division. Perhaps the waterfall would reverse its flow, as there was no doubt that Lou had fallen in love with the East Coast.

Other calls followed from New York. With exuberance, he described Times Square, famously known for welcoming in the New Year and its colorful billboards and tall buildings that could block out the sunlight and not let you know what time of day it was. He relished the presence of diverse people and enjoyed seeing rows of bright yellow cabs during peak hours. His love of music, singing, and the arts drew him frequently to Seventh and Broadway and the many musical stage performances. And to think that he even stepped into St. Patrick's Cathedral on Fiftieth Street with its Gothic arches, as if reaching the sky, and serene stained-glass windows, beaming with colors. Lou … stepping into a church?

This disappearing act kept repeating itself, sometimes for very long intervals—no word at all. At one time, his family thought that he may have died. Hearing from him would have calmed the family's worries. No one in his family, including me, understood that this was part of PTSD. He yearned to be removed from others; he wanted time alone. He needed to deal with his anger, his fight against alcohol, his reclusiveness. He did confide in someone later on that he experienced feelings of unhappiness off and on, and this pushed him to move from one place to another. The last call he placed while in New York was all about his visit back to Greenwich.

Besides psychological concerns, Lou had to tend to his physical health. Several times, he mentioned that he had developed discoloration on his abdomen. During a physical examination, when doctors used a nine-inch needle to penetrate the area, he did not feel a thing in his abdomen. Yet he could feel the sharp jab in another area of his body: his back. Agent Orange caused this effect.

This information made me curious about Agent Orange. I remembered when Lou had told me how Agent Orange was sprayed in the Hue and A Shau Valley areas and how this gave countless soldiers, including himself, blisters and boils. He later mentioned in a letter to me, "It was so bad that even the lieutenant colonel was concerned." Lou also mentioned that many blistered dead bodies were turned in. This is when his left abdomen started experiencing skin discoloration, referred to as chemical burns.

I pondered how chemical warfare can backfire, as in the case of friendly fire. What is shot out gets ricocheted back to its source. It is the same as giving someone contaminated seeds so he or she inherits dead land where healthy crops cannot grow.

Then another long spell of not hearing from Lou took place. The symphony of communicating, then not communicating played on at intervals for years. And the normal questions and fears would restage their appearances among his family members: *Did something happen to him? Was he in an accident? Is he hurt? Maybe he needs money to pay rent. Is he mentally healthy? Is he alive?*

The phone rang one day. "Hi, John. This is Lou."

"Lou, where have you been? We thought you died! What … Reno? What are you doing there? Play what? What is the name of the game? Keno!"

"John, I have been working in Reno." Still trying to make a go in life, Lou had moved to Reno, Nevada, to be a security guard. "You'd be surprised to know that I can play keno. It's a really good game. It's great, brah. You should come out here. And guess what? I have also been hired to do a truck drive. Will call you later."

A truck driver! Little did I know that Lou was into driving trucks.

Another long duration with no letters or phone calls occurred. Then a call came as a surprise to his family who, once again, thought something bad might have happened to him. They were so delighted to hear from him. Lana handed the phone over to me. "He asked if you were here, John. He wants to talk to you. He says he is okay."

"Hey, John. Howzit, brah?" he said.

"Lou, man, we have been worried, worried, worried! Haven't heard from you at all, all this time. I thought you were gone, dead!"

He laughed quietly. "Listen, John, I think I am a wino, living on the streets of San Francisco. My drinking just got out of control. John, I need my wine. That's the only way I can get rid of the nightmares of the war. I am too embarrassed to tell anyone. Promise you will not mention this to my parents, okay? Can you send me some money, John?"

"What? What the heck happened? You could have at least called one of us."

"I just got to get my life together, John." He gave me an address where I could send him some money; he followed this with a short good-bye.

I hung up the phone, deeply understanding what he meant about getting his life together, something that I am still going through since my stroke.

Unlike previous times, within a few months, he called again. "Hey, John, brah … John, I just have to talk to you. Something has happened to me." Then there was a long pause. "Remember how I told you that I lived in the gutters of San Francisco? Well, shit, I got up one morning behind jail bars."

"You what? You were in jail!"

"John, when I asked the doctors why I was there—what I was doing in jail—they told me that I almost killed a guy. I told them, 'No way.' Dude, they had to be kidding. They told me that it was not a joke and that I needed help. So they sent me to a veterans hospital for monitoring purposes. The doctor told me that I needed behavior modification. And I laughed and again said, 'No way,' and that he didn't know what the hell he was talking about. He told me, 'Fine; then don't expect to be released from jail if you don't follow through in our program for your disorder.' So I gave in. Why fight it? They tested me and found my mental ability to be at a fifth-grade level. Imagine that, John—from a high-standing school, now I could only comprehend and read at a fifth-grade level. My teeth need fixing too. They're all rotten because of all the sugar in my wine and drinks. The sugar has decayed my teeth a lot. Brah, I'm just a war-torn, wasted veteran!" I could hear a faint chuckle, yet I knew by the tone of his voice that tears were flowing.

It was in 1977 that Lou began his recovery. PTSD treatment and Alcoholics Anonymous (AA) sessions were introduced to him. This dual relationship lasted for the rest of his life, for this was the sword given to him by his Higher Power to use to chop off the heads of PTSD, alcoholism, and anger. This sword could deal with the compacted glob of warfare atrocities that sat in the back of his mind. He began this battle while he dealt with his skin discoloration and the blood seeping from his left side, which he knew were due to Agent Orange. This war, unlike the others that he had fought throughout his life, was to end in victory. But how would this victory come about?

***

At the end of the next month, another call arrived. "Well, I have been undergoing treatment for my PTSD and attending AA meetings almost every day for now. John, I am an alcoholic! That's what they're divulging to me. I'm so messed up now. But they are going to help me. At least that's what they say at Veterans Services. I am going to get me a sponsor, someone to help guide me and keep me on track. In AA, there are twelve steps that I need to learn about and follow. When I get settled, I'll call you, okay? In the meantime, I will be moving to Los Angeles for my PTSD treatment."

Another call came nine months later. "John, tell everyone I'm okay. I'm still attending my AA meetings on a weekly basis. I found a sponsor and am learning to follow the twelve suggested steps. But, man, these twelve steps are hard. Some readings that I am doing are also helping me. I take one day at a time. I like a prayer called the Serenity Prayer. It goes like this: 'God, grant me the serenity to accept the things I cannot change, the courage to change the things I can, and the wisdom to know the difference.'"

"Lou, that is the well-known prayer of Saint Anthony, so they say. It calls us to do God's will. Many people recite that prayer with deep conviction, not just alcoholics."

"Well, John, I have so much eating me up inside right now. Sometimes I feel like a bundle of nerves. It's been tough—my running away from my wartime nightmares. I try not to complain and just get so depressed, especially when I think of my friends that I lost in the war. So I try to be humorous to deal with it all. Brah, there is so much anger in me for fighting in a war without a plan, besides political and military victory.

"Imagine, I am also finally starting to understand this idea of God. I don't know God at all, except what you and others have shared with me. But somehow I am beginning to look out for this Higher Power. I'm glad you found this Great Being, whom you call Heavenly Father, John, even though you have eccentric ideas of things. But your God must understand you, and I mean *really* understand you, because you seem to know Him in such eccentric ways. Yet how you see Him helps you to move toward Him. Oh, by the way, did you know that I now recite a prayer, the Our Father?"

"What? You are actually praying, Lou?" A light laughter from Lou was heard as he hung up the phone.

After that, whenever Lou came home to visit, he attended AA meetings in Hawaii every week—most times, even three or more times a week—always speaking about steps toward healing. It was important that he be there to strengthen himself. He would say, "One day at a time, John; one day at a time." I had never seen him so committed to life. He went to meetings in Waikiki, in downtown Honolulu, on the beach, at libraries, in hospitals—wherever meetings were held. His AA meetings, along with his PTSD treatment, seemed to keep him on track and motivate him to move forward. And he began to seek out his God with deep humility for the first time. Oh, sure, he called upon God in times of strife during the wars, but he never really knew his God. He hardly attended church as a young boy and seldom mentioned God as he grew up, except in a jovial manner.

I remember him asking me how I knew that there is a God and what God is like. Of course, I was astounded by his sudden, deep interest in God, the Supreme Being. I recall saying to him that He is always there for us, or She is there—that there is no gender in the Spirit. In fact, gender is of no importance in the spiritual world, for we become angels, as stated by Matthew 22:25–29. And maybe the human angels become saints. Or maybe all good angels will become saints. I began speculating, as usual.

To express the love that God has for us, I referred to John's First Epistle, 4:2–3, 9–14; 5:11: "Saint John says to test all spirits, the living and any other form by asking, 'Did Jesus Christ come in the Flesh?'" I said to him, "Lou, the love of God is expressed in this one question. You see, the Holy Name of Jesus Christ is a name of the highest reverence. And the love that God has for us is so endless that sending the Son to earth to suffer and die for us, even before we were born, was to grant each one of us eternal life. This is the price that our Heavenly Father paid for us. Again, when he descended into hell, all the good souls were released into His care and arose with Him. Eternal life is through the Son. One who believes such is of God. John also restates it in John's Second Epistle, 1:7: anyone who denies that Jesus Christ has come in the flesh is a deceiver and antichrist."

Lou appeared a bit baffled. The Good News was still so new to him.

Being eccentric, again, I told him, "Lou, just think: the way to heaven is already open to all of us. And we know God the Father through His Son, who referred to God as His Father. Lou, this relationship is mentioned more than four times in Matthew's gospel, more than seven in Mark, more than eight times in Luke, and more than nine times in John's gospel. But, Lou, if you read the First Epistle of John, he states in 5:7 that there are three—the Father, the Word, and the Holy Spirit—and these three are one."

We also spoke about faith. I recall telling him that we must work for our salvation. Just as we feed our body, we must also feed our soul or our faith. I shared whatever I had learned from many intellectually, scholarly, and unscholarly well-informed, good people and my readings on faith.

As Lou questioned me, I questioned myself at times but in a different way. Little was I aware that he was trying to reach out to God from the depths of his being and heart. He sought to know who God was, where to find God, if God was always there, and how one knows this. He was trying to commit to his Higher Power.

On another occasion, Lou brought up the subject of God again and inquisitively asked where we can find Him—in our hearts? In our heads? Just where is this Great Being called God? I remember saying to him that God is everywhere. "Lou, many people are becoming aware that there is existence in many dimensions of space and time. The space between where you are there and where I am sitting here is occupied by another dimension or dimensions of beings, souls, or spirits. Even if you close your eyes, there is existence in other forms of awareness. And wherever there is existence, there is being, and there is God, the Supreme Being. I remember reading a book, Lou, on how a soul traveled to another dimension and found wandering souls who had already died, reaching out for God also. Try reading books on such things. Many have been written.

"I also have met some people whose mission on earth is to deal with souls of the departed, even to the extent of walking in cemeteries at specific hours appointed by God Almighty to speak to these souls. And if granted by God, they will see them visibly as well, even to the point of sitting together on a bench, conversing, always helping them on their way to God. So God is truly everywhere!"

"Oh shit," Lou muttered under his breath.

"Now, get ahold of yourself, because I have also met people who witnessed departed or deceased spirits in the partaking of meals."

"What!"

"Lou, two people related to me how they heard the crunching of food and actually saw food disappear from plates. But this is something we should not be involved in. We just need to pray for souls. Let God take it from there."

"What the frickin' numbskull are you talking about, John? You lost your marbles or not?"

"Lou, just read the Bible—any Bible. Read the New Testament—Luke's gospel, 24:33–43—and check out where Jesus went after He arose from the dead. Did you know that he ate fish with his apostles? It seems to infer that. You can also find it in the Acts of the Apostles, 10:41, and elsewhere in the Bible." Lou stared at me ludicrously for a moment, and then his jaw dropped.

"Moreover, Lou, are you aware of certain areas on earth that are like portals to the spirit world? I remember reading a newspaper article long ago that stated there are openings or gateways where spirits enter and exit our world. I also met someone on my spiritual journey who shared with me that such things do exist. These gateways or portals exist all over the world in certain regions. I guess if one experiences these types of happenings, one would gain an understanding. No, I take that back. Certain people would understand this, regardless of any experience. Anyway, what I am trying to explain to you is that if God wants to allow a soul to give a message of love or a warning, or even to ask for help or prayers, the departed soul has to reenter the natural world to contact you and exit afterward.

"But be on guard, brother. It's okay but only if God allows a departed soul to reenter! You know how some people play with a Ouija board? Well, it may be a game, but ask yourself who is moving that piece of board if you are not. What you do when playing this game calls upon something or a force without it being God's divine will. Thus, you will have no control over it if it is a negative force.

"Let me share this with you too. When my parents and I took a ride through the countryside when I was very young, we happened to pass a house around a bend. My dad pointed out that the owners moved out because they used to play with this Ouija board and an evil spirit entered their abode and dwelled in the upper corner of the living-room ceiling. It would terrify them and would not leave. No one wanted to buy that house afterward. You see, they allowed an opening for perhaps a wandering evil being without it being according to God's divine will. Souls from all levels and dimensions of existence belong to God alone, and we should never, ever tamper with them. God grants gifts to certain living souls to deal with deceased souls begging for help in order to move them in their growth to His heavenly kingdom. And He also helps the living with certain contacts."

"Hey, brah, don't even say that! No, no need to contact me, please."

"Okay, take all the time you need to ponder what I just shared with you. You don't have to believe it. Afterward, see if you want to reword that same question to me. But God is truly everywhere."

There was no doubt that this visit ended in total disbelief; all you had to do was look at Lou's face. And I thought maybe I said too much too soon. Little did he know that I, too, was seeking out and reaching for God.

Chapter 6

Brother, Where Are You?
Are You Alive?

By 1980, Lou began to conduct AA meetings wherever his travels took him, even in prison. He wanted to make his life useful. That's what he wrote in a book: "Why be alive if you are not useful?" One day, he came home and sadly announced that he had met his cousin in prison. But he was happy to be able to help him in the meetings. "I told him, 'Take one day at a time. You can do it.'"

After further spells of isolation and depression, in 1984, he called from an address on Mission Street in San Francisco. "John, I'm trying to reconfigure my life and put it together from here," he told me. "I want to replace bad memories of myself with good ones." Of his own accord, he was still holding meetings and being of service to others. I thought at that time that he had hit rock bottom—that he had lost everything in life that meant so much to him. But he had finally found some peace in making sure that his brothers and sisters (veterans of war and peace and nonveterans who needed help) got help as well. Without his knowing, others were picking him up, supporting him, and holding him upright.

Again, a vanishing period took place. We did not hear from Lou for a long time. Finally, when we did, he had moved to Wall Street in Los Angeles, a city that he would cherish for a long time. Beating the bushes to cope with his PTSD, continuing nightmares, alcoholism, and a pin in his shoulder resulting from a war injury and seeking to better his life, he kept moving on.

In 1989, he sought help from a day therapy center and attended sessions two days a week for two hours per day, and he went to two thirty-minute sessions of group therapy per week. He tried many types of jobs, such as typesetting, working in security, and proofreading. But his PTSD, battle against alcoholism, chemical burns, and seeping blood resulting from Agent Orange all interfered with his holding on to a job. The red blood blisters continued to form in 1990 and then reached another stage: they began to bleed like water as the thinning blood began to seep out through the pores of his skin. War memories, paranoia, fear, and experiences and thoughts of death all came back to haunt him.

At this point, Lou's anonymous PTSD group sessions were the most effective for his healing, and he stayed committed to them in 1992. This was similar to how he cherished AA meetings as a bloodline. He needed sincere group support—sharing, realizing that many people have similar problems, and learning how to handle them. By 1993, he sought help from the Agent Orange Veteran Payment Program. In 1994, he entered programs at the Los Angeles YMCA on South Hope Street. Within two years, in 1996, he moved to San Julian Street in Los Angeles. In the midst of this, he continued activities as a Democratic supporter and Veterans of Foreign Wars member and even helped at the Good Samaritan Hospital while still conducting AA meetings.

When Lou did call, he again opened up to me about what the wars did to him. He explained why he had turned to booze. He expressed that the nightmares only went away when he drank; that was the only way he could cope with the depravation that war caused him. He emphasized that when he stopped drinking, the nightmares returned. But the nightmares were growing into nightmares of horror, leaving him in an unnerving state. He would wake up in the midst of the horror.

"I dream of what happened with me in the war, but instead of just what happened, it moves into horror. John, I am in the bunker with the enemy rockets soaring over my head. But then the bunker turns into a large freezer with body parts hanging like in a meat market, and I shout, 'Oh f---!' Other times, I fall from somewhere high up, ready to be bayoneted, and my weapon doesn't work. These dreams startle me to wake up in the nick of time." This made him weary and fearful of falling asleep, lest he relive the horrors of war magnified tenfold. He forced his eyes to remain open as long as possible. Shutting them would only open the door to the nightmares of horror.

I shared with him what someone told me to do when faced with sleepless nights: say an act of faith, and bless the four corners of your pillow, asking God to protect you and grant you a good night's sleep.

At this stage in life, Lou was prone to being reclusive and very unsure of himself. He would forget how to love and remember his family. He apologized for that, asking all to forgive him for his shortcomings. His two marriages ended in divorce, and he blamed only himself for it, always upholding the two wonderful women whom he had married. "John, I am having so much difficulty trying to establish close relationships with anyone—my family, my spouse, just anyone! I need to be away from people. I am afraid," he said.

His anger over the treatment he received due to fighting a war in today's world and his suffering from Agent Orange continued. He still felt unsettled because Agent Orange had been sprayed countless times in areas that the troops occupied. Time and again, he kept saying that he was trying to get help. This also meant disability help, as he knew that Agent Orange was enveloping his body. He continuously mentioned the healing steps, talked about books that he was reading, and shared the content that helped him. He must have seen the multiheaded monster that was out to destroy him. But his sword gift would never allow the destruction to take place. He was dedicated to dealing head-on with his PTSD and alcoholism, fighting battle after battle.

During one call, he asked me about the seven cardinal sins and stated that they cause fear but that faith helps you deal with them. And immediately, I thought, *My goodness, is he going actively into Christianity? Lou?* I mentioned to him that we all carry a cross or cardinal sins to differing degrees. Some carry crosses of gambling, some envy, and some gluttony for drugs, food, and what have you. But it is how we carry our cross or crosses for God that seems to count.

I said, "Lou, I remember someone telling me, 'Remember that Jesus fell three times for us and then died.' I think the person was trying to convey to be watchful and to not just keep sinning and do nothing about it.

We must look at the love of Jesus Christ for us, pick ourselves up like Jesus did, and keep moving forward. Lou, these sins thrive on our human side. When we give in to the cardinal sins in the areas of energy, matter, mind, and the Spirit, the results display the marks of evil as well as sins of the flesh. Look at the murders and suicides as a result of abuse of many drugs, especially crystal meth. And then there is mass extermination of humans with the misuse of energies under technological advancements. Further, there is the destruction of human life through germ warfare, which you are well aware of. When we do sin, we hurt God, others, and ourselves.

"On the other end of the spectrum of cardinal sins are virtues. When we interact with the Holy Spirit, we overcome the cardinal sins and become virtuous. Because life is in continuous motion or change in some form or to some degree, moderation is the key to constantly balancing life. Paul's Letter to the Galatians, 5:16–22, clearly tells us how to deal with our human tendencies. Let the Spirit direct our lives toward what our human nature wants, such as anger, greed, and so forth, that our spirit is opposed to; what the spirit wants, the human side is opposed to. When trusting in the Spirit to bring balance to our lives, there is love, joy, peace, patience, kindness, goodness, faithfulness, humility, and self-control."

Years later, I picked up one of Lou's books dealing with alcoholism. He had underlined all the cardinal sins—pride, greed, lust, anger, gluttony, envy, and sloth. I realized that Lou was reflecting on how he could improve his life by dealing with these everyday human aspects.

On another visit home, Lou wanted to just shoot the breeze. We sat and enjoyed talking with one another. We dialogued about how a human being can develop in reaching out to God while on this earth, moving to higher levels of spirituality in comprehending the Almighty. The extent to which he was reaching out to his Higher Power really floored me. It led me to reflect on how catechism was taught more than sixty years prior.

I told him, "Lou, I remember learning about three levels of beings at the beginning of time, with Adam and Eve. There were the supernatural level, angels and above; the preternatural level, before the fall of man—humankind—or the level between supernatural and natural; and the natural level—the present state of humankind."

"Yeah, but going back to the beginning of time with the first humans, what is the etiology or cause of this great sin called original sin, which, in turn, caused the downfall of humankind, preventing them from rising up to the highest level possible?" he asked with great interest, raising an eyebrow.

"Learned scholars throughout the centuries have come up with different possible answers through their etiological studies; there may be more that I am unaware of. One possibility is that evil took on a human form to seduce Eve and then Adam. I wonder if the blame was put on the woman to protect the male pride of the culture when this was written. I honestly think that this also applies to the creation of humans on earth. Culture of the past way back then seems to have shaded the history of the creation of Adam and Eve."

"John, don't sh-- around. What was the second reason?"

"Okay, okay, we can discuss this at another time. Another reason is that evil, being on a higher level than humans at that time, took on a brighter form that misled Adam and Eve into worshipping it. I wonder if jealousy was involved, since the saints, or humans, would judge the angels. That part about saints judging the angels is in the Bible, Lou. It's funny 'cause sometimes humans are referred to as angels. Anyway, maybe because angels never got to have human bodies like the saints did, all the more bad angels or devils seek out to possess bodies to do more evil to destroy humans. Maybe the most evil one also wanted to be God and was jealous of humans, so on the way down to hell, after being cast out of heaven, it decided to destroy God's creation. Boy, Lou, check this out. Beings from two different levels fell here: one from the supernatural to the preternatural and the other from the preternatural to the natural Adam and Eve."

"But, brah, how would you know which it is?"

"Brother, you think I know the answer? I'm not the pope. I don't know. But maybe … just maybe …"

He looked at me, astounded, and then chuckled. "There goes the eccentric one, the most unlearned scholar in such matters!" He roared laughing while leaning his head backward.

"Now, Lou, just maybe—"

"Brah, oh boy, there you go again," he muttered, knowing that I would continue on.

"It would depend on the element of time when the evil force was cast into hell by Saint Michael, the archangel, and, of course, by the command of God the Father. So whatever the reason, it set out to accomplish total destruction of goodness on the supernatural, preternatural, and natural levels in order to reign as chief ruler of hell, a place of total destruction. Therefore, why not make humans worship it, the false Christ—satanic worshippers, et cetera—and as a result, all other humans can easily be misled and fall into the hell of nothingness? Now, when was the best time to do this?

"Lou, many years ago, I went along with my cousin to take his child to be rubbed by a healer. As I continued to go there with him, the healer and I were able to dialogue, just like you and me, about things in a comfortable manner. One day, this healer told me how he reads the Bible. Now, this healer is close to ninety years old. The healer went on to say how he read in his ancient Bible he had brought over from Portugal that when Jesus came in the flesh, Saint Michael, the archangel, battled in heaven with the evil one, who was another angel very close to God. Gee, God must have loved this thing once upon a time when it was a good angel. But because Jesus was on earth, this evil one sat upon the throne of heaven. Here was an angel filled with the cardinal sin of pride on a spiritual level, if such does exist. Man, what an anomaly!

The healer went on to say that Jesus commanded, 'Get off the throne!' from earth. By permission from the Father and the Holy Spirit, Holy Michael, the archangel, and all the holy angels cast the evil one and its fellow angel followers out of heaven, having to travel through the many dimensions of existence to the depths of hell for eternity unless they repented. It is here, or on the way down, that they must have lost their beautiful glow of spirituality and become hideous, eternally self-destructive within and without, ugly beings. Hey, beware, Lou; rather, be on guard, because evil can also change and appear so beautiful, as bright as an angel, only to deceive and destroy us. That's a reason to test all spirits. And evil can quote the Bible inside and out. But it is incapable of doing a holy act for God. By choice or blindness, I don't know.

Anyway, this eccentric guy is thinking that this battle in heaven might have taken place during the creation of humans, and certainly before and even continuing while Jesus came to earth. This is when the final expulsion from heaven took place. So in order to descend into hell to save us, Jesus, one with God the Father, had to take on a lowly, humble human form, even below that of angels, to suffer and die for us, paying the full price for each of us. It is the death of Jesus that flung open the gates of hell. He was pure light of essence—cosmic energy, whatever you want to call it—not a surface, bright light of appearance as evil is. You know, Lou, I did not read about any saints being in heaven before Jesus arose from the dead."

"Really, John, there were none?"

"Nope. I don't think so. Unless I missed it somewhere. If you find it, let me know, brother. So the souls, as Matthew's gospel says, were in hell until Jesus died and broke the chains of hell to release them. There was only hell! And then, only then, did the saints rise with Christ. As I mentioned in the past, the saints must have been in a limbo state of sleep, since they led decent or close to holy lives so that even evil could not touch them in hell."

"John, wait, wait. Hold on. Hey, brah, hold on. You also said earlier, unless they repent ... these ugly, damn destructive beings of souls! How the hell would you know?"

"Well, I really don't. But ... but when Jesus reached the age of manhood back then, he was tempted three times in the wilderness by the followers of the evil one or the evil one itself, probably on their way down to you know where. Lou, read Matthew 4:1–11. After each temptation, Jesus would say to it, 'Man shall not live by bread alone but by the Word of God. It is written, thou shall not tempt the Lord, your God. Only God shall you worship!' Bull's-eye! You will live by God's Word. Do not tempt your God; only your God shall you worship! Eh, brother, don't you think it would get the messages?"

"Yeah, real blind and undiscerning. But, John, why didn't Jesus just destroy them then and there?"

"Maybe because He had emptied Himself of all His godliness, coming down as a lowly, humble human being made even a little lower than the good and bad angels, according to Hebrews 2:5–9. In so doing, God, the Holy Spirit, needed to remain in heaven. As a result, this gave time for repentance to all in existence."

"Those evil bastards knew that!" he shouted. "And that was why He was tempted by those ugly things. What cowards, picking on Jesus because He humbled Himself for us. Shoot, He was even lower than they." For a moment, I was stunned by Lou's reaction. "Say, John, tell me about how Jesus emptied Himself of all His godliness."

Again, I was stunned. My God, Lou was really interested! "Okay. Lou, do you remember where Jesus was born?"

"Yeah, but all I remember is that He was born in Bethlehem and that there was a star that led three wise men to find him."

"Well, go back in time to a stable, to Luke's gospel, 2:1–19. Jesus was born in a manger, covered with a swaddling. He was not born in a hospital. There were no doctors, nurses, or clean bed and sheets. There were just His mother and foster father, Joseph. Oh, and some animals."

"What kind of animals, John?"

"What! What kind of dumb question is that? Now you think I'm a historical veterinarian? Hey, remember, brother, I am the unscholarly one!"

"Well, brah, you better listen to the Holy Spirit and not get so frickin' hotheaded over my question. After all, you always start up these eccentric conversations," Lou responded, smirking.

"Okay, okay, the animals were most likely from the horse, cow, and sheep lineage. Hey, Lou, did you know that some people believe in a legend that says on Christmas Eve, the lineage of animals that was present at Jesus's birth faces the East where He was born and bows—or kneels—in adoration? Apparently this is supposed to happen at midnight."

"What!" he exclaimed in almost disbelief. "Where the hell do you come up with these ideas?"

"Lou, I did read about it in several sources and met someone who swears on the Bible that it is true and who actually witnessed it. But it has to be witnessed without the animal sensing your presence. Shucks, I stayed up till almost midnight one Christmas Eve watching this full-grown, adult white horse grazing in an empty lot next to our house. I was watching it in the hope of witnessing it face the East and kneel by folding its front legs under itself."

"Wow, holy shit! Really, dude? And … what happened?" he asked with his eyes wide open.

"I don't know. My snoring woke me up. And it was already past midnight. Sorry. Shucks! And to think I tried so hard to not let the horse know that I was watching it. I kept peeking through the Venetian blinds. I wonder if the horse saw the blinds move. But I made sure that I moved them slowly just to have a tiny opening to peek through. It was an all-night watch. You know, I tired myself out trying so hard that sleep overtook me.

I think the horse must have had a good laugh over human frailty." This left us both chuckling.

"Man. Dude, going back to Jesus's birth, that's pure, ultimate humility on God's part! Wow, Jesus is the epitome of benevolence," he commented while shaking his head in disbelief over the lack of discernment by negative influences.

"But, brother, bear in mind, regarding the repenting concerning the three temptations, that they were strictly between the evil beings and God. Because evils are out to destroy us totally, we just need to rebuke them in the Holy Name of Jesus, the Christ, who has come in the flesh. We have to remember to live by the Spirit and not be controlled by our humanness."

"Shoot, there is so much to learn. John, on that first sin—that is not how the Bible is written. I recall people saying that the fall took place with Adam and Eve and an apple, you know, like Snow White and the seven dwarfs with the poisoned apple. What the hell am I asking?" he said, chuckling.

"Lou ... Lou, I just thought of something!"

"Oh sh—here we go again."

"You know what? That apple in the Garden of Eden might have stood for temptations to rule a kingdom—hell—along with its keys, given by the evil thing to Adam and Eve. And they gave in to the temptations. The temptations were probably along similar lines of deception to those faced by Jesus. You see, Lou, when Adam and Eve gave in to the temptations and fell, the gates of hell were sealed and locked all souls in bondage, chained in hell. The evil one now had a kingdom of its own with human slaves—hell. It sat upon its own throne in hell. So now there would be no saints. But it also wanted the throne in heaven too. Why? Because it felt it could do Jesus under, thereby destroying all that is good—the reason why it sat on the throne in heaven until Jesus commanded it to get off. This command must have come from Jesus when He was on earth.

"Then the exodus from heaven took place with the evil one and its negative followers being all cast into hell by Saint Michael, the archangel, and all the holy angels. This exodus from heaven could have expanded over many dimensions of time and space. Damn, it dared to even tempt the Lord our God, Jesus Christ. It was desperate to stop the crucifixion because if it didn't, it would lose its keys to the kingdom of hell, it would lose human souls, and the saints would awaken, which is exactly what happened when Jesus descended into hell. That is why it tried to tempt Jesus and also tried to stop the apostles and others from allowing the crucifixion to happen!

"Remember, Lou, Jesus emptied Himself of all godliness, lowering Himself below even that of angels. Now, being on equal ground with all humans, including Adam and Eve, Jesus could counteract the evil force by entering hell through the human death of His body. After Jesus suffered tremendously, was crucified, and died, He descended into hell. His being composed of the purest light of complete innocence removed the darkness wherever He walked throughout hell, lighting His pathway with His holy, pure, cosmic essence, and claimed the souls to take them up into heaven.

"So now, hell is totally subject to God the Father. Yes, Jesus Christ has come in the flesh and now is in eternal possession of all keys to our Heavenly Father's kingdom. The battle continues, though, until the end of time—the final judgment—remembering what Jesus said to His tempters: 'Only God alone shall you worship.' They have their time, the tempters, devils—or fallen angels—and demons—fallen humans that worship the devils. It really doesn't matter as long as repentance is there—sincere repentance. So the battle continues until then. One can wonder if Jesus needs to walk through hell consistently in order to raise the souls who are working upward. But not so for those who lead a life of holiness, as He already broke the chains of hell so they can freely raise up to God the Father. Would these need a second judgment?"

"Brah, it makes sense. Somewhat, a little, maybe …"

"You don't have to agree, you know!"

"Okay, okay, I know that. But wait, wait … How the heck do you know what is important in your faith with so many changes that have taken place in all aspects of life?"

"Let me put it this way, brother: in the early 1960s, many different denominations of churches underwent change for the sake of updating practices to bring the faithful closer to God. This included the Catholic Church that convened in Vatican II in Rome. While this was happening, evil took advantage of it with secular humanism. What should have remained in the area of clinical psychology found its way into the educational system, the workforce, and all aspects of society, including churches.

"The me-myself-and-I psychology took over common sense. Values clarification, which was meant for clinical patients, was rampant in schools. No values, character traits, or morals were taught. There were no references to what was right or wrong or gray. Freedom of choice without any foundation permeated all walks of life. This amoral culture of self eroded the fabric of society in America, which continues today. The results saw a tremendous increase in family dysfunction, divorce, substance abuse, subliminal messages in music, and devil worship and a decrease in family and personal values. The pendulum swung from one end to the other and missed the middle point of moderation. Corporal acts, spiritual works of mercy, beatitudes, and gifts of the Holy Spirit were shoved backward into the shadows. That's why there were so many problems! No one was left back to watch the ranches. The good news is that these spiritual behaviors are stepping out from the shadows to the forefront again, trying to bring balance back into our daily lives. Now, time is needed to heal a nation."

"So what else happened?" he asked impatiently, tapping his right foot on the floor.

"Traveling even further back in time, in order to keep updating the Bible, throughout the centuries, sometimes the writers of the Bible created explanations out of sync, not in sequential order. Some wrote to just give an explanation as to what happened. In this process, some concepts have changed while others were repudiated due to cultural perspectives at the time when the Bible was going through a cycle of being written and rewritten. The misapprehension of biblical concepts could have easily occurred. By now, there're probably fallacies or misunderstandings in every single church denomination on this earth—unintentional, of course. As evidence of our human shortcomings, things can easily be twisted by writers, interpreters, and even readers. That is why one must ask the Holy Spirit for guidance when reading the Bible.

"Some concepts may be incorrect, but the important thing to remember, Lou, is that Jesus broke the chains of hell because of God's love for us. Souls that wanted to go to God were forgiven and released from the depths of hell. You know all those different levels that were there. Hey, be happy; we got a chance to go to heaven to be with Jesus Christ. Remember!"

"Really, you just wish, John!" He chuckled.

"Regarding updating, in one church, the Apostles' Creed was replaced somewhat with the Nicene Creed. The Apostles' Creed is what contains all the truths of our faith, which are the most important facts of our belief—you know, like the infrastructure of a building. Christ did descend into hell. He did it to release the souls waiting to rise with Him. *Savior* is truly befitting of Him! And we will have a resurrection of our spiritual body or being. That might be related to why God wants the saints—and Lou, remember, that's us—to judge the angels."

"Me, judge an angel, let alone be a saint? Hell, you have got to be kidding. Yeah, I guess at least we can hope, John," Lou responded laughingly, almost spilling his glass of soda.

"Lou, some Christians wish that churches would include a prayer calling upon Saint Michael, the archangel, and all the holy angels to do God's will and protect us from all evil we battle daily. Anyway, Lou, a friend of mine said for me to get ahold of books that are not included in the Bible of today because I may find them interesting."

"But still, how do you know what to believe?"

"Well, my dad once reminded me to only believe what comes from Jesus. So, in a way, I really believe that the Catholic Church is the one church in direct line with Jesus because of Peter, the apostle. This authority to carry on when Jesus left this earth was given directly to Peter by Jesus. Lou, you will find this passage on the establishment of the church in Matthew 16:15–19—that Peter will lead and whatever is bound or loose on earth will also be so in heaven. Moreover, evil will not overpower the Church of God even though it tries to. John's Epistle, 20:21–23 and 21:15–17, states how the 'Holy Spirit is to guide them, in forgiving, and not forgiving (that which is inherently evil), and to care for all who believe, who suffer and are persecuted because of their belief,' and so forth. So it is here that the Bible and the Apostles' Creed have connections."

"Brah, if this is the true church, the so-called Catholic Church, how come there are so many other churches on earth? Look around—so many different churches: Pentecostals, Lutherans, Methodists, Assembly of God, Baptists, Good Faith Churches, Mormons, Seventh-day Adventists, Jehovah's Witnesses, and many more."

"Probably because God created diversity among all human creatures in their thinking, attitudes, experiences, and individual perspectives. Other churches or Christian denominations, also diverse in their own ways, are therefore needed to act as support channels to address the differences of people and lead them to God. We all worship the same God, you know. The gospels bind us together as believers in Jesus Christ. The Catholic Church was and will always be there because it was founded by Jesus while He was on earth. He prepared Peter and the apostles to carry on after His death, I guess until the end of time."

"Okay, okay, get back to our point of origin, that preternatural level! How high can we go?"

"Lou, wait! I have to tell you about this. My nephew shared with me about a book that he read concerning people with strong and bright auras that lightened their beings. I have also witnessed people with strong electromagnetic fields that remained untouched by negativity. Perhaps some humans can soar high above the natural level while on earth. Maybe all can. Elijah did, and most of all, the aura of Jesus at the transformation or transfiguration is proof that we, as humans, can reach the preternatural level, or at least try to."

As time went on, whenever I said, "Lou, what do you need?" he would always respond, "Don't worry, John; I am fine. I don't need anything." He didn't want to be gluttonous toward material things. But I would send him some things, and he would be grateful. Lou continually reminded me to accept people just as they are, saying, "If they are not hurting you, it's okay, John. Even if you disagree with them, it is their right to think differently. Why let it bother you?" And so my tolerance for others grew, just as his did. He also taught me that when we try to control others or depend on them, we create suffering for ourselves as well as them.

It was then that Lou wondered about my reaching out to God, reading the Bible to learn about the lives of saints and their authored works, and seeking others and speaking to them to learn. I explained to him that as he was searching for help for himself and others dealing with PTSD and alcoholism, I was doing the same but dealing with visions and visitations.

Chapter 7

Natural ... Spiritual

One day, Lou asked me, "Say, John, what's going on in your life? Damn, you are really an eccentric, you know." His face had a sincerely inquisitive expression as he waited for a response.

"Lou, I always had to deal with these things, and not understanding spiritual experiences, you either live in fear or in awe. You just know that you need God and some guidance to get you to a level of understanding why this is happening, what the meaning of it is, and what you are supposed to do. There is a strong awareness of the unknown. It will linger until you find direction."

"What kind of experiences are you speaking about?"

"Brother, as a young child, I had a dream of Jesus sitting on His throne upon a cloud, with a crown of gold on His head. He appeared in His white garment with a red covering draped on one of His shoulders. As he drew closer to me, I could see the shoulder-length, dark brown hair, but His face was not clear, just hazy and cloudy with illuminating brightness. Not a word did He speak. He simply smiled as He gazed at me and blessed me with the sign of the cross. In my dream, I knew without doubt that it was Jesus. Because it was a dream, I didn't give it a second thought. I thought this happened to everyone—that it was just something normal.

"But later on in life, when I was fully awake, a vision of the holy mother, Our Lady of Peace, was granted to me in the heavens. She was standing with her arms outstretched, with rays of light flowing outward from her hands and toward my own image in the sky. It almost threw me! I thought, *Surely I'm imagining things.* But as the rays from her hands continued to shine outward, the Most High then showed me many tortured souls. Some of their faces were twisted, while others displayed much sadness and blankness. So much agony was reflected in their faces. And then a monk, dressed in his long robe with his hood on, stood holding an open book. This image remained for some time, and then the vision ended.

"During all of this, I kept wiping my eyes, looking away and then turning back, testing myself to see if this rapture was what I was truly witnessing. Was it my imagination? It was truly real, as were the details. Although I had a vision in a dream at a young age, which I thought common for anyone, this experience shocked my whole being, as it occurred while I was fully and consciously awake. Moreover, a person sitting next to me was not aware of what was going on. Visions can capture your whole being, which you are unable to communicate to another person at times. This experience also taught me that some people will be able to see a vision while others will not, no person being better than the other—just different missions on earth.

"Lou, gosh, visions can jerk a soul. As an earthly soul, exposure to a spiritual realm kind of tears your being apart due to the starkness of being in two different realms of existence at the same time. It's just like what you are going through, Lou. You need a sponsor to help keep you on the right path from alcoholism to sobriety so that you can move forward and maintain a balance in life. I needed a spiritual director to help keep me balanced among the natural, preternatural, and supernatural or spiritual— that is, until we both can become independent of such and begin to help others as well. So I sought out help. This was in April 1971. I directed my search to obtaining help from people who I thought were deeply spiritual in their connections with our Heavenly Father, who could be trusted and believed in. I also sought out others who experienced visions."

"Brah, how did it go? Did you find someone?" Lou asked.

"Well, no one really understood this in those days, during the 1960s and '70s. And it was taboo to speak about such things. People, including some of God's ministers, were afraid to speak out on this subject. One with the knowledge of dealing with such warned me not to talk about it—'Quiet, John; don't tell anyone. Don't mention it at all. Just pray'— and he would hurry me out of his office, lest anyone see us. And I used to wonder, *What am I supposed to pray for?* He didn't tell me that for every one of these experiences, I would be made to walk through hell for God. I learned this as I was actually walking through the bashings of hell while simultaneously reading the writings of saints.

"One minister tried to help me, but I don't think he understood, and maybe he didn't even believe me. But at least he tried to help me. Other devoted servants of God guided me to read books on the saints. It was amazing to find sincere people who were willing to help, even not knowing what in particular to address. These people were like angels sent to just be there to hold me up. I was unaware of how mysteriously God works at times. I also met Christians from different denominations who exorcised and helped souls to God Almighty. On the other hand, 'Emotionally disturbed, mentally unstable' echoed in the background of the paths that I walked. Even from those in whom trust was embedded, the ugly monster known as jealousy peeped out from behind its green walls to attack and destroy. And then I realized why that one minister warned me of such. He, too, must have walked the same path that I was walking."

"John, I never even sensed this about you ..."

"It's okay, though, Lou. I think people with similar experiences travel similar paths. I'm not sure. Christians know that God has a reason for everything. I learned so much from those who dialogued with me, and even from those who pushed me aside. Those who pushed me aside forced me to seek out others who were willing to share. Now that was a blessing in disguise. Because of that, I met others who were able to teach, share, and help me to move forward. 'Seek, and ye shall find' (Matthew 7:7 KJV).

"You need to know, Lou, that these spiritual experiences should not be asked for. They should strictly be God's will. You will walk through hell and be constantly attacked from all sides and in many ways. But it is for God, so that is fine. And God will walk with you or carry you through hell. Remember when I told you about the dream I had of our Lord? Well, that was the beginning of walking through hell. For many years after that, whenever I was in a semiconscious state upon awakening, I would not allow myself to be awakened out of fear of feeling like an ugly being, which hovered like a dark shadow beside me. I would call upon Jesus and then force myself back into a deep sleep. This went on for many years. Stupid me, I thought it was normal! *Learn to live with it!* I said to myself. But there was this tug in me.

"In my quest to learn how to handle all of these things, I met a person who told me outright to open my eyes, confront it, and not be afraid. Well, I finally did such. So with fortitude and holy anger—like, *How dare you bother me, for I worship only God alone!*—I did not allow myself to escape back into a deep sleep. Calling on Jesus with my whole being, I opened my eyes. I was ready to rebuke the fear in Jesus's name, but it was gone and has never returned since. Lesson learned: have no fear. Have no fear, for Jesus is with us! James 4:7 tells us to submit to God, and the devil will flee from us. And the First Epistle of Peter, 5:8–10, guides us to be steadfast in our faith in calling upon Jesus Christ."

"Damn it, John; I didn't know that you were going through all of this and, with all else, ending your medical career and adjusting to having a stroke. I just don't know how to help you. In fact, I was hoping that you could help me. I'll be—"

"Lou, there is a reason for all that happens to us. In the struggle to find spiritual assistance, I learned so much and met so many Christian soldiers, fighters, and warriors and Christian guardians and servers of the faith. Through the grace of God, I met a sincere couple that shared their God-given gifts with me. They related the following predictions between 1968 and the early '70s, which have come true—at least most of them.

- Jews will accept Jesus, but not necessarily all.
- Russia will be converted if people continue to pray the rosary, or the message of Fatima.
- The wall will be broken. (In Germany, the Berlin Wall fell in 1989.)
- Science and technology may go beyond their limits and try to play God. (Cloning, stem cell research, unnecessary space exploration, and inner-earth bombings resulting in earthquakes, tsunamis, and climatic changes have occurred.)
- New diseases will come about—some with cures, some incurable. (Ebola, HIV, flesh-eating diseases, bird flu, and swine flu have arisen.)
- There will be a Third World War, but it will be fought differently and will last for a long time. (See the September 11, 2001, terrorist attacks in New York.)

- We are judged daily. Is hell now on earth?
- A time will come when nothing will move and nothing will sell, though many will try to sell things. (See the global financial crisis, with 2009–2012 being the rock-bottom years.)
- Marriage among those committed to ministries will be allowed with others in God's service.
- There will be famine upon earth. (We need to learn about sustainability and taking care of ecosystems.)
- Green will begin it all. (Maybe this refers to the greenhouse effect.)
- Some will have a death wish and pray to die rather than live.
- There will be no political parties in America. People will vote only for the candidates who can do the job in order to lead the country forward.
- Evil Satan will be let loose on earth. (Look at the four marks and the lack of values.)
- Encounters with the spirit world will rise and increase.
- The magnetic poles of the earth and its fields will be altered. (Follow the earthquakes.)
- There will be attempts on the pope's life and the prophecy of the last pope.

"It was also shared with me that books on prophecy, such as those of Nostradamus and Saint Malachi, would be of interest to me."

"Holy shit, some of these things have happened already and are happening or should be happening soon, if what you're telling me is true!" Lou responded.

"That's not all, Lou. God has everyone on a mission here on earth: you fulfill your mission on earth as you live your life to best please God. Let me shake you up!"

"Huh? What, John?" he remarked with confusion.

"Lou, I decided to put in writing some things that would help others so that they, too, would find out what God asks of them. Some souls know clearly what to do; some need guidance. I first wrote in 1973. Maybe others can write also and share what they have learned. Even though there may be diverse opinions, beliefs, and thought processes, the common factor is service to God. Sharing among diverse writers helps to validate, correct, and elevate both the conceptual and emotional intellects, truths, and traditions.

"I continued to find help and wrote again in 1984 of my thoughts about changes taking place in churches. I continued to learn from God's and others' help. I knew that one day I would write again. Then in 1989, I included dealing with spiritual confrontations in my master's paper on affective and moral development at university. Well, three professors asked that I remove that portion because they lacked the knowledge to deal with it. They said that they were not theologians."

"John, the Eccentric! Man, I can't get over this. But hey, brah, can you send me a copy of it? I would like to read it."

"Okay, let me put it together and decide which version to send you, or what would be easy reading."

"Thanks, huh, brah!" Lou said, and we parted.

At the time, little did I know that Lou was moving up through his so-called healing steps. He would just say to me that he was doing some deep self-reflection that was revealing his limitations and he was now beginning to admit his faults. He was attaining a form of peace as he was accepting people as they were because he had opened up to his own faults. He said we can do this as long as no one hurts one another. He sounded so saintly!

Lou didn't want to come home unless he knew how to act, being so unsure and doubting himself. He didn't want to burden his family. He wanted to have the funds to pay for things—food, entertainment, and the like—so his visits, even short ones, only occurred when he felt confident in himself. When asked where he would like to live—Hawaii, California, or New York, his three most frequented places—if he had a choice, he always chose East LA. He saw his fellow veterans there as his brothers.

I joked with him on the phone one day and said, "Take care of your fellow humans. Some of them may be direct descendants of Jesus."

"No way. Mary did not have other children!" he yelled.

"True. Now—"

"There goes the Eccentric. Bye, John," Lou interrupted, and the phone went dead.

At this time, little did anyone know that Lou was on medications for Agent Orange exposure, type II diabetes, a skin disorder, kidney failure, and lung problems; the medications included nitroglycerin, lisinopril, lovastatin, metoprolol, ranitidine, and aspirin. He was a walking medicine cabinet. He had intermittent bleeding on his left side, which he sometimes described as "pouring out like water." He continued his medical treatment and other treatments at the Veterans Affairs Outpatient Clinic on 351 East Temple Street in the heart of Los Angeles. This is where his heart grew in loving humankind.

Then Lou went through another spell of PTSD. We did not hear from him for more than two years. We thought he had done so well, and here again, the PTSD was driving him backward. By this time, his grandparents and parents had died, leaving him somewhat alone with his two brothers, their families, and his sister.

For the sake of his siblings, as they looked up to me as their uncle—me being the same age as Lou, who was much older than they—I sought him out. In order to find him, I decided to write letters to all addresses where he had lived, asking the apartment managers for assistance in giving him my letter. I provided each with a return envelope. I even included a pen in the event he did not have one to respond to my letter as well as my phone number. In East Los Angeles, a manager responded to my letter and called me, stating that Lou had moved out but that there was another address for me to try. With great excitement, I followed up on the new address. Unfortunately, he had also moved away from the new address, and no one knew where Lou went from there. It seemed that all was lost. I really thought at that point that my buddy, my friend, and my brother was gone and that I would never hear from him again.

Desperate, I called the American Red Cross. I then discovered that if you know the person's name, birth date, and social security number, you can check if the person is deceased. What a thought! But it had to be pursued, as no one knew his whereabouts. What a relief it was when it was reported that the deceased didn't include Lou's name!

And then about four months later, out of the blue, Lou phoned. That was a shocking surprise. I said, "Lou, where are you? How are you? I thought you may have died!"

It sounded just as before, like a tape-recorded message, when he had finally left active service. "I'm okay, John. I just needed to get my life in order again. It is a continuous battle. But it is okay. I'm trusting in my Higher Power."

I did wonder if he had found God. Here, he admitted that he was trying to better himself with help from his Higher Power. It was not ostentatious on his part. *Hmm ... hmm, his Higher Power?*

He then detailed how he continued his treatments with the VA treatment centers and moved whenever he felt uncomfortable. As always, he found great satisfaction in helping his fellow veterans by conducting AA meetings, but he was not proud of his instability in doing things. Lou also relayed how he was so proud that he had celebrated eighteen years of sobriety. And then he invited me to visit him.

"Where do you live, Lou?" I asked him.

"On Skid Row, brother, in East LA! I love it here."

So, in 1996, I set out to meet Lou in East LA with my son, who had had a terrible reaction to drugs called ice and pot. Because I wanted to spend time with my son at Disneyland, we stayed at a motel in that area. It was the time of a little girl's passing, which was all over the news media. Hearing about such a young life stolen so quickly deeply affected my son and me.

Because Lou lived on Skid Row, he told us what bus to board and where to meet him. He was there at the bus stop when we arrived on Eleventh Street. With inward pride, he escorted us to see his apartment at the Ellis Hotel, which was adjacent to a park area with a basketball court on Sixth Street. He had a clear view of the court from an upper-level floor. From his window, we could watch the players dunking basketballs right into the nets through green tree leaves. Lou stated that right below us was where he held AA meetings to help his fellow veterans.

I met some of Lou's fellow veterans, who also lodged there with him. The drawn lines on their faces carried the sleepless nights, the sufferings of trying to face daily life, the anger, the disappointment, and the physical and psychological injuries of war. Yet, like Lou, they carried the pride of fighting for their country—for American freedom. Like Lou, I, too, felt that these veterans deserved so much more out of life for dedicating themselves to our country, the United States of America.

After enjoying his tidy and attractive apartment, with two red, yellow, white, and black ceramic clown faces from Goodwill hanging on a wall, we had breakfast at a simple restaurant located near his bank. He seemed to enjoy the Mexican influence and poured the hot red salsa all over his eggs. He spoke to us about staying sober and things he did to help himself, hoping that my son would hear this and it would have a positive effect in helping him. And it did.

After breakfast, Lou took us to the area he had bragged about: the garment and fashion district. He happily showed us the shops. I was surprised! Having visited there in 1962, when the most residents were Caucasians who spoke English, I saw that most shopkeepers were now Mexicans or other Spanish-speaking people. I did not understand a word they said as I moved from shop to shop. I felt as if I was in Mexico. I was glad Lou was there to interpret for us. It was then and there that I really understood the phrase "America, land of the free." Here was a true example of that and the importance of learning foreign languages in schools across America. It felt so different than it had in 1962.

Afterward, Lou took us to the library in downtown LA. He was so proud of the Los Angeles Public Library, with its colorful and artistic dome standing out among the buildings of downtown Los Angeles and Bunker Hill. We went in and saw the vast array of books occupying the shelves, many of which he enjoyed reading there. And at his insistence, we enjoyed an ice cream sundae in the library's restaurant. He then guided us along the pathways of the beautiful library gardens, snapping pictures along the way.

The Los Angeles Public Library, Lou's favorite stop.

Afterward, we toured an underground shopping mall close by, chuckling at Lou's humorous remarks now and then. Lou needed to get medication there, but he didn't say what it was for—his heart, lungs, kidneys, diabetes, or any result of his years of service. He suffered in silence now.

Before my son and I left, he gave me a book by then President Clinton. Because he was a dedicated supporter of the Democratic Party, Lou had been invited to the president's inauguration. And during the holiday season, the White House sent him a beautiful Christmas card. He was so proud of this that he gave it to me to keep, even though he knew that I was a Republican in name only. I have always voted for the best person, regardless of what party he or she belongs to.

Lou just wanted to show my son and I a good time in East LA. And it was a very good time. He was proud of his accomplishments and his desire to serve others by conducting weekly AA meetings wherever he resided. The meetings that he conducted were open to all active service members, veterans who had served during wartime and peacetime, veterans who were disabled or homeless, and anyone else who needed help. He was also proud of his readings and writings, and before I left Los Angeles, he reminded me to send him a copy of my spiritual confrontations, as I had shared with him earlier that I was writing about my spiritual experiences.

Upon returning home, thinking of his meetings, I sent some home-grown Hawaiian coffee to Lou. He was so appreciative to receive something from back home. It gave his AA buddies a taste of Hawaii. And every Christmas, I sent him a card with prayers offered to him. He sent me a photograph of himself and wrote, "From an aspiring writer, poet, lyricist, wit, or any other semit buffoon." That was Lou—turning things into a smile or joke, regardless of how serious a situation may be.

***

While helping many veterans recover from alcohol and drug addictions, while at the same time helping himself, Lou's life was threatened twice. Maybe it was because loan sharks and drug dealers were no longer making money off of those he had helped. Once in downtown Skid Row, an attacker came up from behind him. It was a good thing that Lou used a walking cane with a knife at the end of it because he was able to use it to ward off his attacker. But that didn't stop him from helping his fellow veterans. But now many of those he had helped were moving away from Skid Row to a better life. He had no one to turn to for help when faced with negative encounters.

He continued his PTSD treatments and held AA meetings for alcoholics and drug users, and again, his life was threatened. Finally, we discussed the necessity of moving out and finding a safer place to live. It was no longer safe for him to remain there in Skid Row. To my surprise, Lou listened and actually did move.

Before his move, Lou phoned me directly. "Hey, John, any other spiritual confrontation happening with you?"

"Are you all right? Do you know what you are asking me?" I asked him.

"Of course I am. I really am interested, John."

"Well, Lou, I did have another one a year ago but did not want to burden you with my concerns because you had more than enough to carry on your shoulders."

"Hey, John, I'm okay. Don't worry. I just want to hear about what you go through out of curiosity, among other things."

"All right, Lou. If you say so. I did have another experience that occurred on a Sunday, in February, 1981, close to midnight. As I was driving home from a hospital on an outer island, I saw black lightning bolts streaking down from the top heights of heaven to earth. These were intense, jet-black bolts against the black of night. Can you picture that? The bolts were so jet-black that they stood out against the blackness of the night sky. And the jet-black lightning bolts remained in a permanent stance for a while. I sensed that it was not a good sign. Man, I was shaken. Being somewhat bewildered, I called a friend as soon as I arrived home and was told to look in the Bible. By the grace of God, Luke 10:17–18 said, 'And the 70 returned with joy, saying, Lord, even the demons are subjected unto us in thy name. And he said unto them, I beheld Satan fallen as lightning from heaven.' I then realized its meaning. It was evil in the form of lightning falling from heaven. A few days later, another person confided in me that he, too, saw it. Then I knew that I was not going nuts. So I continued my search as to what to do."

"Did you find an answer?"

"I think so. I just rely on God, the Holy Trinity, now."

"But don't you think all denominations of all Christian churches on earth need to put up a good fight in this battle against evil on earth?"

"Yes, there are so many energies surrounding humankind. A prayer to God asking to release Holy Michael, the archangel, and the holy warrior angels to help us on earth would help. Maybe a prayer to Saint Michael, the archangel, would return to all church services or something of that nature." Our phone conversation ended with inner peace for both of us and for his upcoming move to a better place of residence.

Lou moved to Ballington Plaza in Los Angeles in 1997. This was a step up for him, for now he had his own private bath. That meant a lot to him. It was there that he started to converse more with others. He would write and say that he enjoyed just sitting outside with other tenants, shooting the breeze, surrounded by beautiful plants and colorful flowers and green shrubbery.

Me, in an early morning picture taken outside the fragrant entrance to my building, where meals are served to seniors, including yours truly. This shows a delightful everyday experience. Who said there is no God? Not me!

Before long, he was up and about again, this time moving to the veterans home in Barstow. Wherever Lou moved, he would send me pictures of his apartment. He clicked his camera in every room—the

kitchen, the bedroom, the bathroom, and the entrance to the apartment—
as well as the outdoors. And he never failed to send a picture with himself
looking in the mirror, waving while taking a picture! Of course, one could
only view the camera flash in the photo and his hand waving at you. But it
added much humor to his photography skills, and you could almost hear
his chuckle while taking the photo.

The photographer's view of the washbasin from the great seat.
No need to close the door here. I still couldn't figure out the flash.
Brains are not my strong point. Maybe humor is.

Lou was becoming a changed person. He saw the goodness in people
and did not let others' shortcomings interfere with his treating them with
respect. He started to accept himself, and he showed a happiness that had
not been seen for a very, very long time.

By this time, his overall health was failing, especially his heart. His
heart condition first showed its signs in 1992. The heart pains continued
and worsened while he was in Barstow, but he still kept on with his PTSD
treatments and helping his fellow veterans by holding weekly AA meetings.
He never gave up, for he knew how hard it was to give up and deal with bad
habits and the tragic effects of alcohol, drugs, and war. Lou was somewhat
unaware that he was being a true server. He mentioned once that there
were so many soldiers, easily into the thousands, he had assisted as he had

been fired upon and had returned fire as he dealt with the wounded, the injured, and the dead in many night-defense and ambush positions and in moving in and out of helicopters. He continued, "I really need my therapy, John. I want to grow old gracefully, if I'm fortunate enough."

When he called from Barstow, we would laugh over his daily morning walks in the desert, as he called them. "John, I'm just watching out for them snakes!" he stated in horseplay. "It is so hot and dry here. Just arid land all around you with some sparse greenery here and there, and cactus plants. But there is something nice about it. You just have to get used to it." And then he would continue on about trying to get disability help for his failing body and war-shot alcoholic recovery. But he must have enjoyed living in Barstow, for he even volunteered time at a high school there.

Barstow.

Our next conversation opened with excitement.

"John, I found a book that is just my favorite size to read, and it is of tremendous help to me. It is *The Little Red Book* by the Hazelden Foundation.[1] Did you know that we become wiser through pain and problems? Now, I believe in faith and prayer. Things are beginning to

[1]   Hazelden Foundation, *The Little Red Book* (Center City, MN: A.A. World Services, 1986), 39, 62–63.

happen because of faith and prayer. I am beginning to overcome my fears because I am beginning to understand them. As the book states, 'Fear is nothing more or less than a distorted faith in the negative things of life and the evils that might beset us.'"

"Right on, Lou. This destruction happens because fear is a weapon of that which is negative or evil. Lou, you sound like a Christian. What church do you belong to now?"

"Wait, John, let me finish. We have received a spiritual reprieve day by day through God because we turn to Him for help and are thankful and we give unselfish service to others. Service to others is the key. One day at a time. Prayer helped me see how I was, and faith showed me that I had walked the talk. And finally, because I realized that, I can, in turn, truly help others. I no longer have that fear, like you, John. Remember how you had to overcome fear? It's the same. It is amazing how fear can destroy a person's life."[2]

"Hey, brother, you certainly have come a long way!" I said with amazement.

After a short laugh, he quickly stated, "John, hold on. Alcoholism is an illness, a disease, a poison, and for me, it is also genetic. But, John, turning to my Higher Power, faith, and prayer; doing the will of God; being of service to others—these are what keep me on the road to sobriety. And, John, I am so grateful for the sponsors who helped me reach this point in my life. God does work in mysterious ways. And I am also learning to deal with my PTSD at my sessions at the Veterans Administration."

"Lou, you really sound like a Christian. Brother, you are a Christian. The will of God is what governs every Christian. Charity with acts sustains faith."

As usual, he respected what I said, whether he agreed or not. "John, I just pray that my life is pleasing to my Higher Power so when it is my time, I will enter those pearly gates of heaven on Judgment Day, greeting Saint Peter with a joke."

"Watch out, Lou. Saint Peter might beat you to the punch. By the way, Lou—"

"Oh no, now what, John?"

---

2   Ibid.

"You know, since Jesus already opened or destroyed the gates of hell, Judgment Day may be every day that we live on this earth; that's what some of us think. Look at it this way: some of us are greeted by an angel, a relative, a friend, a saint, or even the holy mother or Jesus Himself when we leave this earth! Why do we need to be judged and greeted again? The final judgment will be when the lost and vile souls, and you know who those negative beings are, are dealt with by God Almighty. You don't have to agree with me; you know that."

No response for a moment. "I really don't know what you are talking about. Will call you later," he answered. The only sound I heard afterward was the dial tone.

Chapter 8

Hello! Hey, God ... Is That You?

By 2000, Lou decided to visit Hawaii. It was not meant to be his last visit. Maybe he knew it might be. He enjoyed morning walks in the green, lush valley of Hawaii. In his pocket was his pedometer. He made sure that he took care of his health and kept up with his AA meetings. He admitted that he could easily slip if he didn't. Surprisingly, after one of his walks, he brought back a big box full of custard-filled and haupia-filled (or coconut custard–filled) pastries. That was Lou—always bringing smiles and delight to others. His brothers, his sister, and my family just gobbled them all up. We had such a great time with him.

One day, he asked me to take him to clear up relations with some special people in his life. At first, I didn't think anything of it. I just thought, *Well, that is good to do to live a good life. We need to forgive and make amends.* I drove him around in my blue car as he paid visits to make long-awaited amends and heal relationships. "Cleaning up his life" is what he called it. "I need and want to practice acts of kindness, courtesy, justice, and friendliness," he said.

One afternoon, Lou called me over to his parents' home. We sat on the porch to shoot the breeze, as we always had in the past, just enjoying the simple things in life. As birds came by, tweeting loudly, we threw bread crumbs on the ground, much to the little creatures' enjoyment.

"John, tell me more of my Higher Power, even if it is contrary to what others may say," Lou said to me. "I may disagree with you, as I have in the past, but sometimes, something might just click for me. Tell me more about your God."

"Lou, it's *our* God. God is simple. In fact, God's simplicity has made creation so beautiful."

"Really, John? Then what is your stance on creation and the book of Genesis?"

"What stance is there to take?" I said. "Creation is God's handiwork through the processes of science. One day of creation could be equal to seven or even ten million years of science. Remember how people wrote the Bible from their perspective during their time. I really don't see any contradiction between God and creation, or science, for that matter. It is we, humankind, who make God so complex. Remember, you don't have to agree with me."

"Are you saying that you don't believe in miracles?"

"No, God certainly performs miracles that totally defy science and natural laws. God even uses natural laws to defy themselves—i.e., winds to part a sea. No doubt, these timely events exemplify that God is at work. Lou, I guess what I mean is that all creation and humankind are from God. If we do not take care of both with vigilance and prudence, humans will be the losers. Here is an example; I met a person on this subject also."

"Sh--, I just knew you would say that," he said, chuckling.

"But it is a truth, Lou. And I bet many others have probably discussed it also. If a bullet, when fired from the chamber of a gun, displaces the air, can you imagine what a rocket can do when it displaces the equilibrium between earth's electromagnetic gravitational pull and its outward centrifugal force? One rocket, hmm, not too bad of an effect. But consider many rockets and other space paraphernalia being launched into outer space, and from many nations. Why are asteroids heading toward earth? Is global warming only the result of CO_2 concentration? We, humans, are responsible for what is happening out there, and here on earth as well! Look at the bombs that are sent up into the upper layers of the atmosphere and down into the layers of the earth or the waters, the methods of discarding chemical germ warfare, and many other acts in the disguise of testing. Many of the aftereffects have not as of yet been conceived."

"Okay, okay, Brother John," blurted out Lou. "By the way, I always meant to ask about the appearances of the mother of Jesus. She appears as

Caucasian in the West, as Asian in the East, as black in the South, and as cosmopolitan everywhere else. I have seen her depicted in different ethnic races. What gives, dude?"

"Hey, would you want to appear as a wolf in sheep country? Would you be able to relate to the sheep as a big, huge wolf?"

"Shoot, all the sheep would be running for their lives! Brah, there would be no relating going on," he replied as we both chuckled. "Ha, okay, you have a point there, my friend." He continued smiling.

"Lou, how would you inspire them if there was no relationship to ethnic appearances? Hey, brother, let God do His thing."

"Speaking of animals," Lou remarked with a twinkle in his eye, "after you die, what would you want to come back as—a wolf or a bird? Wait, wait, now, John; how about as a bug? Would you want to return as a bug?" he asked with a big grin.

"You mean reincarnation, brother? You know, Lou, I don't understand reincarnation, but hell, if I was stepped on and shoved around all during my lifetime on earth, you think I would want to come back as a bug to be stepped on or slapped around again! Another lifetime of that sh--! Hell no! Just leave me in peace with our Heavenly Father, the Holy Spirit, and the Son. But now, if you had said a king or a prince, well, that would be another story," I forcefully uttered as we both laughed hysterically, almost falling out of our chairs.

And the rest of the time was spent on other talk that only friends can make and share without being demeaned by one another—talk about the love of God, how to help others be self-sufficient, and eternal happiness.

"Lou, did you know that Jesus gave us the greatest gift to last a lifetime for each of us on this earth and in the next?" I asked him.

"What are you talking about, John?"

"Remember God the Father's will to open hell for souls to be raised up into heaven?"

"Shoot, what about it?"

"Well, at the Last Supper, Jesus created the everlasting pact with humankind. He took bread, broke it, gave it to His disciples, and said, 'Take and eat it, this is My body which is given for you. Do this in memory of me' (Luke 22:17–20). With the cup of wine, apparently, He did the same and said, 'This cup is God's new covenant sealed with my blood which is poured out for you, for many, for the forgiveness of sins' (Matthew 26:28). Brother Lou, Jesus said to do it in memory of Him. So every time we consecrate the bread and wind—sorry, wine—into His body and blood, and every time we receive Him in communion, sins are forgiven. Hey, that includes ours too, you know."

"So what, now you're going to receive Jesus daily?"

"Hey, why not, brother? At least we *know* that we'll make it to heaven, and also those for whom we pray too."

It was clear that Lou sincerely accepted each individual just as he or she was. He would say to me with candor, "John, as long as a person is happy and doing their best, it's okay. Even if you disagree with them, as long as they are not hurting anyone, it's okay." And, boy, did he disagree with me on many things. At least I think he did, for he would just nod as if to say, *That's okay, if that is what makes sense to you.* Human tolerance had developed tremendously, and I followed what he shared.

***

Lou wanted to get a second opinion on his health condition's treatment at another clinic. Shortly after his return, he moved back to Los Angeles in 2001. "My heart pains are worse now, John," he told me. "Just took another angiogram, and a new treatment was recommended."

At this time, we entered into World War III on September 11, with the terrorist destruction of the Twin Towers in New York's Financial District. This led to a totally different type of warfare than was ever known before. I remembered what two people had prophetically stated about this war in the late '60s to early '70s.

Lou wrote to me later and stated he was afraid that we were entering into a war of wars that would last as long as the Vietnam War. To add some lightness to the situation, I simply shared, "Well, some say that we are on our last pope or soon-to-be last pope from readings on prophecies. But, of course, prophecies are fulfilled only in God's time and not ours."

Lou responded, "There goes Eccentric John!"

He continued his treatments, ran weekly AA meetings, volunteered to help when no one else would, and did his best to serve others. His group therapy sessions still reaped positive results for him; they provided the ability for all to share, to help one another, and to push for the benefits that all veterans deserved. And as time went on, disabilities that were service connected began to become factual.

Lou moved again, this time to Long Beach, California. He seemed happy there, for a special relationship started to develop. He would visit the library there, something he always did wherever he lived.

Ring … ring … ring. "Hello, John, is that you there?" Lou answered when I called him one day.

"Of course, it's me. Who did you think it would be?" I answered in a witty sense.

"John, I am going to send you my will," he said. "If anything happens to me, can you take care of everything for me?"

"Hey, of course, my brother." I responded, and I borrowed his famous phrase: "Don't worry."

By November 2002, Lou called and said that he needed to undergo surgery. "Looks like they will need to remove one of my kidneys, John. They also found a spot on my liver." There was reason to worry, as he had had a stroke two years before.

We spoke about what would happen if it didn't go well. I became candid with him and related how the soul leaves the body with the light at the end of the black tunnel, the soul exiting its physical form, and how the new life is seeing, hearing, and feeling but without the body. "Lou, there is no distance to travel, no time to worry about. You remain alive but without the physical body as we know it." We hung up the phone in a peaceful manner.

The surgery to remove his kidney was successful, and Lou then seemed to find a new turn in life. Or so we thought. Somehow, other health issues unexpectedly sprung up, and before we knew it, he was moving again in June. But this move was different. It was to find the nicest place possible.

Still waiting to hear about being compensated for his disabilities, Lou took the initiative to write again. In his notice of disagreement letter dated March 24, 2003, he states,

> With the above disabilities and another 10% for diabetes mellitus type II, and the removal of one kidney due to Agent Orange, I feel I should be compensated at the 100% rate, after

all the years of hand to mouth existence, seventeen honorable years' service, five years' Vietnam combat service, being rated 90% and paid at 40%. IT FEELS UNJUST. Thank you for the consideration.

Respectfully,
Lou

On May 20, 2003, Lou received a letter stating that he was to be granted full payment of the 90 percent disability and to no longer be paid at a 40 percent disability rate. Overjoyed, Lou made his last move. It was a special move because he was about to receive what he had been fighting for. He was also moving for access to better health care at his favorite place: the Veterans Affairs Outpatient Clinic on 351 East Temple Street in the heart of Los Angeles. Most of all, he was moving on up to the Museum Tower Apartments on Bunker Hill in Los Angeles.

On June 14, 2003, he proudly entered his abode. He kept raving about how beautiful it was, being connected to a mall with a soft, calming, and cascading waterfall over tiers of curved steps in the daytime. At night, it became a stage for plays and other performances.

The waters would stop to allow it to be a stage for performances.

"There are also different water fountains, John. One is long and slow moving; another has six tiers of water cascading down. Even across the street in the business buildings, there are figurines with water fountains." He expressed how all his life he had sought to live in a place like this. It was his dream come true, as far as lodging was concerned. He felt as if he was moving way up. And he was not ashamed to have his son and daughter-in-law visit him in October. He felt like a Donald Trump or an Oprah Winfrey in his own little reality. And I thought, *What, a disabled veteran getting paid now at a 90 percent disability rate, feeling like a millionaire or more? Wow!*

What also made it special was that when Lou went to the YMCA on Hope Street, he could view the colorful gold and bluish artistic rooftop of his favorite place to visit: the Los Angeles Public Library. And, of course, he had to get his Los Angeles Public Library card. It was there, in Los Angeles, that he continued his association with the Midnight Mission, exercised at Bally Total Fitness Center downtown, and did his share with the American Legion.

Back in March, Lou had called and said, "John, can you please pick me up at the Honolulu Airport in June? I want to come back for my class reunion." He was so excited and looking forward to this event tremendously. He wanted me to go with him.

I told him, "Don't worry. I'll drop you off, and you just enjoy yourself. When you are finished, I'll pick you up. And, Lou, I am putting my writings together for you to see and read when you get here. I just need to reword and update things to make it clearer." I got a draft copy ready for him so that when he came for his class reunion, I could hand it to him. I wrote, "To Lou, the Veteran. From John, the Eccentric." It was a positive time in his life.

In May, he called with disappointment in his voice. "John, I am unable to come due to my health. My health needs attention for now." If he had any worry at this point, he tried not to let it be known. "I am also getting ready for my son's visit." He was very exuberant in making this statement, as he hardly saw his son at all. This was a new beginning for them. He wanted to make his apartment nice for his visit to develop a lasting, loving father–son relationship.

On August 8, medical personnel called to inform us that Lou had been rushed to the veterans health center on East Temple Street in downtown LA. His condition required that he be admitted to the veterans hospital in West Los Angeles, close to the airport. Lou called and, as usual, said, "I'll be okay. Don't worry, John." Because I happened to be getting over the flu, he added, "Take care of yourself." And I intended to call him again.

Chapter 9

Our Higher Power

On Friday, August 15, 2003, at around noon, the call came in from the West Los Angeles veterans hospital. Lou's sister had just finished cleaning the house. I happened to be visiting to check on the family. Seeing tears running down his sister's face, I grabbed the phone and continued the conversation. After hearing the doctor announce Lou's passing at the age of sixty-eight, I heard her state it was important that someone come to claim Lou's belongings and his body.

It took time for all of us to internalize what we had just heard. Many calls were made after that, first to Lou's family members. Afterward, things moved quickly. How could Lou's wishes be carried out? We rushed to the bank before it closed. We got there just in time to get Lou's will out of the safety deposit box. The metal box felt so cold, as if to say, *Life has ended on this earth.* It is ironic that no matter how well funerals are planned out ahead of time, gaps of blankness still occur when it actually happens.

The next step was to reserve flights to LA to claim Lou's remains. After being able to get a compassion fare seat and set things in order, three days later, I was ready to board the plane, with my antibiotics in my pocket, to retrieve my friend, my buddy, and my brother.

Before this could occur, calls came in from the Doheny Eye and Tissue Transplant Bank in Los Angeles and the transplant line in Orange, California. Even in death, Lou wanted to help others. He had agreed to donate his eyes and body for use in medical research or education or even for transplants. Then I was on my way to Los Angeles, Lou's favorite place—the City of the Angels.

At 5:00 a.m. on Monday, I arrived at my destination, LAX. The morgue would open at 7:00 a.m. In order to wile away my extra time, I caught a shuttle and rode around LA from San Marina, where a loving Asian family was dropped off at a simple but attractive white house surrounded by flourishing greenery. Afterward, we moved on to Echo Park. Here, a young man, who one could detect was spreading his wings, met his welcoming, happy mother. We passed views of Hollywood and Universal Studios as we headed to West LA.

It was a chilly walk down the empty, too-quiet corridor toward the morgue. My footsteps echoed throughout the entire ground floor. The keeper of personal effects was not there yet, as it was 6:45 a.m., so when I heard footsteps shuffling, packages sliding, and doors slamming, I deeply sighed with relief. Retracing my steps to the double steel doors at the end of the icy tunnel, I claimed Lou's wallet, credit cards, keys, bankbooks, et cetera—all that is needed to carry out one's legal will. Add to that his walking cane. I then had to walk over to the Family Care Department, thinking along the way, *How will I get to his apartment? Where is the bus line at this veterans hospital?* Well, with my bad knees, I could use his cane. That Lou—he even thought of me in his passing. A tear of thank-you ran down from my left eye.

Arrangements were made to have his body cremated and his remains returned to Hawaii. His ashes were to be given over to Hawaii's ocean waters. Lou had wanted to give his body to UCLA or USC medical facilities for research to help others. The educational medical institutions close to the veterans hospital were contacted, but to our surprise, and I bet Lou's also, they would not accept his body because he had not appeared in person to will his body over to them and sign the papers while he was alive. Due to this oversight, the receptionist at the Family Care Department helped to make arrangements to have his body cremated so that I could return with Lou to Hawaii.

The mortuary manager was kind enough to give me a ride to Lou's apartment. Upon arriving at his apartment, I saw two huge puddles of bright red blood—one in the bathroom and one in the kitchen. Evidently, his left side did its final bleeding from Agent Orange here. After cleaning up his apartment, I began to disperse his belongings in a manner that he would have wanted and as stipulated in his will.

Lou's furniture was given to the community in Long Beach, California, that had helped him a lot in his health and faith. His personal belongings were given to his buddies in Barstow, who had fought with pride for their country and who continually gave deep meaning to the American flag. Other cherished items, such as his many books on AA and his tokens depicting his years of sobriety, were being prepared to be distributed to the humble souls at the veterans health center in downtown LA and the YMCA on Hope Street. Lou would have wanted this in order to encourage and motivate others to keep up the twelve steps so they could, in turn, help others. This would cause an endless movement toward sobriety. His token marking twenty-five years of sobriety was kept for his son.

In the midst of carrying out his will, I came face-to-face with all Lou had shared with me during the happiest time of his life, just a few months prior. Lou had been declared a 90 percent disabled veteran in November 2002, giving him payments as such in February 2003, for him only to pass on in August of that year. The increase in his disability benefits had allowed him to move to the Bunker Hill area on June 14, 2003. Here, he was surrounded by all that he treasured in life: the music center, the Museum of Contemporary Art, the beautiful water fountains, a fashion center, the business center, yellow cabs, and the beautiful waterfall outdoor stage.

One evening while there settling his effects, I had the privilege to watch a Chinese fan-dancing performance on the stage that served as a waterfall during the day. I pictured Lou watching it alongside me, for he loved performances, going back to his high school days of stage acting. He was so proud of a street next to the apartments that was named for General Thaddeus, a name he shared. He always had a good laugh over this fact whenever he mentioned it to me. Besides that street, I took in the roof of artistry and colors above the library from high on Hope Street in Bunker Hill, a spot that he had described with much pride.

The YMCA on Hope Street in downtown LA held its weekly AA meeting. It was about eleven in the morning when I arrived to bring closure regarding Lou's demise in response to a request from some of the members. A beautiful woman with shoulder-length brunette hair spoke first and said how she had been clean for twenty-five years. I admired her honesty and was proud of her fight to overcome the ravages of alcoholism. She shared how difficult it was, as all recovering alcoholics know, dealing with her family and friends, but she hit twenty-five years of being clean. All in attendance were overjoyed for her, while at the same time thinking they could do it too. What an inspiration to everyone! Lou was just about twenty-six years sober at his death, another inspiration for those who wanted to implement the steps of sobriety in their lives.

Then, I asked if I could address the group. Tearfully, I announced that Lou had passed on.

"Uh-oh!" screamed a man from the other side of the room. It was an older man, wearing a light beige jacket and a gray hat, who blurted out, "Oh, I have been looking for him!" After the initial shock of being told of Lou's passing, leaning on his cane, he found his way over to where I was seated. "I even went to the front desk of the apartment building where Lou lived and asked for his social security number to be able to look him up. I was so desperate, wondering if anything had happened to him. And, of course, the desk clerks would not release Lou's social security number to me." And so he prayed and asked God to help him find Lou. "Lou and I would walk to the AA meetings together, with him living directly across from my apartment on Olive Street." He looked at me and, in tears, said, "You know, the last time I saw Lou, he gave me a green plant in a nice vase and said, 'Here, take it; it is yours.' With it being so nice, I told him that he should keep it in his place—that it was too nice to give away and he should make his place beautiful with it. But he insisted that I take it and keep it. He knew—he just knew that he did not have much longer to live!"

After the initial shock over the announcement of Lou's passing, we all prayed together in a circle, which was probably how they normally ended their AA meetings. I gave out Lou's books on alcoholism and tokens for years of sobriety, thinking that Lou would want me to give hope to those whom he had delivered the message to. And that is exactly what I said as I handed out the books and his medals of sobriety—that he would want them to keep sober as they moved on with their lives and, one day on their journey, be of help to others in the same illness.

As I looked around, I saw how Lou had touched the lives of many men and women of all ages and from diverse ethnic backgrounds. A few young

African American men and Caucasian men came forward to grasp Lou's merit sobriety medals with tears in their eyes, and I repeated that Lou would have wanted me to give the medals to them on his behalf. Later, a young woman came up to me accompanied by the older gentleman. Both were in tears and said how Lou had given them hope to continue moving forward, and the gentleman blurted out, "Oh, thank you, God; now I know what happened to him. I kept going over to his apartment for us to come to our meetings together, and no one knew what happened to him or where he was."

A coordinator from the health center in downtown Los Angeles also called to say how the veterans there needed closure for Lou's death. I couldn't deny them that. Lou would appreciate it. That was his favorite place. So along with his nephew, who joined me later, we trotted to the health center in downtown Los Angeles, Lou's second home. That is how he felt about the place, the people, the veterans, and the workers where his heart was, in LA.

About forty veterans were present from all walks of life, bearing the scars of war, the hardships of life, and the fight for survival in a nation of freedom. A few veterans from Barstow were trying to make it over. Some veterans from Long Beach also arrived to join the services. They had a huge picture of Lou on a table with candles on both sides of it. The closure that was requested began with a humble prayer. A fellow veteran then played "Taps," after which each person, one by one, gave testimony to Lou's efforts in helping them and others to move on in life. It was touching, as so many shared how their lives had changed because of Lou's caring for his fellow veterans and even nonveterans.

One veteran spoke loudly. "Lou told me, 'I can't stand you, but I'll help you out.' He even gave me money when I needed something to eat." And he laughed just like Lou. "Can you imagine? Yep, he said, 'Man, I really can't stand you, but here's some help.'"

Before we left, a young woman came forward, stating that she really needed to talk to me. "I never knew that an alcoholic can change to be a nonalcoholic until I met Lou. You need to know that all my family members are alcoholics—my parents, my brothers and sisters, and even my husband. So I believed that that's it; it's just how we are. We can't change. But Lou showed me that it can be done. Now, we have hope." She handed me a white ceramic smiling Santa Claus mug. "I want you to keep this. I always treasured it," she said. I thanked her and stared teary eyed at the mug, and I understood why she treasured it. It looked just like Lou, with its beard, mustache, and even the eyebrows, along with that twinkling in the eyes. For a moment, I felt that I was looking right at Lou. And then I remembered how Lou had written to me and sent me pictures of himself playing Santa Clause for Christmas parties at places where he lived. I could not help but chuckle.

Some of Lou's friends expressed how they would miss him and how he had filled their spirits, given them hope, been an inspiration and an example of dedication for them, and walked with joy upon this earth. They thanked him for his giving nature and gave him the following messages.

- "I will even miss you when I get older."
- "I have years of being straight because of you. God bless you."
- "You always share from the heart."
- "Thanks for filling my spirit."
- "He had Santa Claus eyes, a beautiful smile, and a warm heart."
- "He taught me that people with any type of abuse can recover. I thought there was no hope for me or my family."
- "You always brought a whole lot of recovery to all. Your spirit will always be with us."
- "May God bless and keep you until we meet again. I learned a whole lot from you."
- "I appreciate your dedication. Your life is a testimony to God."
- "Thank you for your love and tolerance."
- "Thank you for sharing your spirituality."
- "You walked in joy upon this earth."
- "You shared hope with so many others."
- "You were and are an inspiration to me and many, many others."
- "We will meet again in heaven and have a good discussion."

In the will that Lou had sent to me a year earlier, he first wrote that it was all right to be buried in the family plot. In his last letters, he stated that it would be fine to scatter his ashes, whether in California or Hawaii, or be interred in the ground. The veterans who knew him well assured me that Lou would want his ashes scattered.

Early on Sunday morning, I attended Mass at the Cathedral of Our Lady of the Angels on West Temple Street. It was a high Mass with incense and blessings. Somehow, heaven knew that I would be there on Lou's behalf. The deacon's singing was like that of an angel. His voice was strong, and the message sung uplifted all present in the high-ceilinged cathedral to spiritual heights.

I followed the crowd after Mass, somewhat out of curiosity, down the stairs and into the mausoleum, and I was surprised to see my favorite actor, Gregory Peck, interred there. Lou must have had a good laugh here, seeing me say out loud, "Hey, that's my favorite movie actor." I chuckled along with him.

The Cathedral of Our Lady of the Angels on West Temple Street in Los Angeles.

That afternoon, Lou's nephew and I rode in silence in the shuttle to the LA airport. After passing the Staples Center and arriving at our destination, with empty hearts, we boarded the plane and returned to Hawaii with the ashes of the fallen, stalwart veteran warrior in our arms. Knowing Lou, and having full charge from his family to carry out his will, I began the arrangements for Lou's funeral services in a way that he would have wanted. We would place his ashes on a table set up on the sand with a review of his life in colored pictures. To give some uplift to it all, leis and flowers would be provided in a container. They would go on the table as well. The army needed to be notified so that they could play "Taps" and do the rifle salute. The American flag would be handed over to Lou's son; Lou would love this. A minister would give a short service. (I didn't think Lou would be particular here, so I planned to ask a good priest or minister to perform the services.)

His ashes would then be scattered offshore in the waters of Waikiki. The paddlers would ready the canoe, with his ashes to be held by his son, and he would be taken out to sea accompanied by a catamaran for others to ride alongside him for his final journey. When we were out there, another short prayer service would be said, with Diamond Head in the background. His son would then slowly lower his ashes into the ocean waters of the Pacific. And to top it off, Lou would want everyone to be happy. We hoped that a really nice wave would form so that the canoe could "catch a wave" coming in. This would bring laughter to everyone. It would also be his final laugh—his final performance. Humor was a sign of life for Lou. And I wouldn't forget my writings for him to read, but now in his new life form.

I asked Veterans Affairs for a burial allowance, as a veteran's status must be checked first. One clerk gruffly remarked to two others in the office, after looking up Lou's status, "Shit, the bastard had one foot in the grave, and they finally declared him 100 percent disabled!" I wonder if Lou was aware of this. He would have been overjoyed.

A letter arrived stating that Lou was not considered to warrant a service-related death and that six hundred dollars was all that was allotted to nonservice-related deaths at that time. Well, this eccentric friend fumed and wrote letters, stating how Lou had given his life to help many soldiers in wars and many homeless and disabled veterans after war, how he had been attacked twice because he had helped many veterans to move on from their dealers, and how he had suffered from bleeding blisters. The letters also included all the effects he suffered from due to Agent Orange, besides his war injuries and his being paid as only 40 percent disabled after being declared 90 percent disabled. As a result of the trail of documentation on his service-related disabilities (something that Lou and all the veterans in his groups stressed to one another to have on hand), Lou was finally given the allotment for a service-related burial.

It was only after Lou's death that I decided to learn more about the Vietnam War. I watched news clips and movies and read articles on anything about Vietnam and tried to vicariously experience what Lou had gone through. Newspaper clippings gave me further insight into why Lou had turned to drinking and why he had wanted to remain in LA to help his fellow veterans and other people. I felt the agony of what Lou meant when he said he knew what was about to happen there on Hamburger Hill.

By this time, the reality of what happened at My Lai was out in the open. People pointed out the atrocity of such an unjustifiable act, during which an estimated four hundred to five hundred innocent men, women, and children were slaughtered. There was no reason for this to have happened. It now occupies space in history books.

I tried to find out if Lou was part of My Lai. He never stated if he had been part of it, witnessed it, or dealt with the overbearing stench of almost five hundred dead bodies. But whatever happened must have been traumatic, for it just ate him up. He would get up in the middle of the night and sit up in the dark, sweating profusely and holding his arms as if a rifle were in them, as he yelled, "Charlie, Charlie!" Then I realized what many veterans go through and why Lou wanted to help other veterans.

Good-hearted people sent their sincere expressions of sympathy. Two of Lou's former classmates mentioned in their expressions of sympathy that they cherished memories of Lou's role as the emperor when they were in a high school play. They were connected to the play and had fond memories of its production. One of his classmates stated that pictures of it had been turned over to the school archives.

September 13, 2003

It was a beautiful morning. The sun's yellow rays shone down from above while the blue skies draped the heavens. The gentle tropical breeze did a flowing dance, so picturesque and characteristic of Hawaii. Lou's ashes were held inside a green ti leaf wrap placed inside a carved wooden container, which rested on a table on the white sands of Waikiki. Color pictures of his life and his famous Santa Claus smile stood next to the urn, along with a coconut woven basket full of colorful flowers. The flowers came from the leis, which had been de-strung to protect the marine life.

His final performance began. Prayers were given, accompanied by singing. "Taps" was played, sparkling army rifles were raised, and shots rang in midair. After being folded so neatly, the American flag was then given over to Lou's son.

Then the veteran warrior took his place with his son in the canoe for his final voyage. As the elite brown carved canoe and catamaran took leave from the sandy shores and glided outward over the vast blue-green sea carpet of Waikiki, forces of life were in movement with each wave, to and fro. The energy of life continued but now in a different form. Diamond Head sat in all her queenly majesty to recognize the stalwart veteran warrior as he passed by her mountainous volcanic slopes. And with compassion, she served as his magnanimous memorial marker.

In a moment in time, the ocean stood still. It welcomed the veteran warrior into its crystal-clear, lukewarm waters. In synchronization, the vibrant flowers in green, pink, red, yellow, and white were sprinkled with care, floating with love as a canopy on the water's surface.

Diamond Head is shown in the background.

The wave formations starting to grow in the far distance could be seen moving in on the horizon. And as the canoe, with the spirit of the veteran warrior, moved to return to shore, time was on its side. Before the canoe reached shore, the waves raced with a simmering, gracious rhythm to catch the canoe and lift it high up into the air! And there was loud laughter, much delight, and tremendous joy as Lou, in spirit, left the passengers' side and rose up to meet his Higher Power, chuckling!

Peace be unto you.

Writings

To Lou, the Veteran.
From John, the Eccentric.

On Spiritual Confrontations

From my 1973 writing:

A taste of the supernatural is indeed pleasant, or it can be of a revolting nature. When it is so pleasant, it can mislead one easily into "ego adoring ego" until it blinds itself and no longer sees its Creator, our Heavenly Father. Evil is indeed cunning, particularly when one tries with all sincerity to serve God, thus the importance and need of a spiritual director. Such neglect could result inevitably in the service to oneself, eventually to self-destruction through prolonged states of soul torment in discerning the meanings of spiritual confrontations, being preoccupied with, Why? What to do? How? When it is so revolting, fear of the unknown and stages of depression may set in and increase with depth as time lingers on—self-pity. In addition, if the experience granted is of the "awful," a fear far beyond the natural realm must be coped with.

From my 1989 writing up to the present (Lou, I omitted my 1984 writing):

What is the nature of these confrontations? How does one deal with them, or distinguish true ones from false ones?

As a minister recently shared with me, in dealing with God's realm on earth, we all have a role to play. Like on the battlefield in war, some of us, as spiritual warriors, are front-line warrior fighters; some are fighters in tanks, ready to move in; some are in the air, on the waters; some are doctors, nurses; others are psychologists and healers. Then there are those who do the strategic planning, while others are coordinators, cooks, those that dispense linen, clothes, artillery, and guards. And there are many other roles. But whichever role you play, keep steadfast as a soldier of the Lord, without any fear.

We must rely on the Lord, Jesus Christ, to show us the way.

Spiritual Confrontations May Occur in Three Different States

1. **Full consciousness:** Having control of all the faculties of the mind (reasoning, perception, memory, freedom of choice, etc.).
2. **Semiconsciousness:** Having control of all the faculties of the mind, as in full consciousness; however, the body remains in an inert state, like on the threshold between deep sleep and wide-awakeness.
3. **Unconsciousness:** Being asleep in a dream state. It is said that we should not believe in dreams; however, visions in dreams are of another nature. Use discernment here.

Spiritual Confrontations May Occur in Five Different Forms

1. **Meditations or contemplations:** Voidance of oneself so one is able to unite with the divine will. The fewer distractions, the better; all people who meditate are aware of this. Many saints experience this to the highest degree.
2. **Visions:** Experiences that may leave a person in awe or in fear, depending on their source. Visions may appear in regular hues or as illuminations of bright white, gold white, and blue white. The whiter an illumination is, the higher in spirituality the entity or source exists.

   People who have shared their visions with me have stated that their visions have occurred through sight—supernatural, angelic, or preternatural—of a departed one; through sound, such as in talking to someone; and through touch, or feeling the other entity touch them. The latter examples start to move into the area of visitations.

For example, a woman told me of her mother's passing. Just before her last breath, her mother had a big smile on her face and then expired. Even though there was no wind that day, the curtains gently moved, fluttered open, and then closed.

This is similar to the writings of those who describe various mediums used by God. A priest shared the following with me from a book that he read, *Mystical Theology* by Durrant,[3] which listed three mediums.

I.   **Strictly supernatural**
II. **Divine touches:** Vibrations, nebula, flashes, wind.
III. **Natural:** Sensible, corporal, bodily.

Having experienced such things and heard about them from others, I would describe such experiences as the following.

I.   **Supernatural level:** Above the natural realm.
II. **Movements of different energies:** Divine in origin; expressed in a somewhat natural manner at times, such as through touch and wind, visible and invisible.
III. **Natural level:** Seen with and experienced through bodily senses.

Also, a combination of levels could occur, such as an occurrence is invisible and yet the presence is heard, felt, or both.

Visions may be seen through the senses or through the intellect. Sense vision may at times be deceiving. The rule of thumb in determining the source of visions, which I learned from someone who had visions consistently, is if the resulting force thrusts the soul toward goodness and the glorification of God, then it comes from a good source. Teresa of Avila gives more value to intellectual vision: "Intellectual vision is more of certitude, bringing greater

---

3   Durrant, *Mystical Theology.*

interior benefits and effects to the soul in going about in peace
and desiring to please God."[4] In other words, because of its
understanding or somewhat of an understanding, serving God
has more of a direction—a spiritual thrust or yearning.

Readers must know that even though good visions are from God
Almighty, they should never ask for them or desire to follow that
path. That opens up another path that the soul may not be able to
handle. I have found that souls who are granted such would walk
through hell to do God's will. This is the same as Judas Iscariot
did to accomplish the holy will of the Father, and it's the same as
those who help other souls find their way to God—for example,
helping drug users on ice move toward healing. You, too, will
walk through hell. Only God knows how much an individual
can handle, and He allows us to take certain paths. He is always
with us, no matter how many times we have to walk through hell.
Saint Teresa of Avila warns us of such and expresses how we must
be humble and on guard, as one can easily be deceived. Even the
imagination's desires can lead one to see or hear what isn't really
there or dream about what one desires. Most of all, she states, "The
trials suffered by those whom the Lord grants these favors to, are
not few, but extraordinary and of many kinds." Therefore, "the
safest way is to want only what God wants."[5]

3. **Visitations:** A visitation by a spirit, or specter, be it good or evil,
can leave you in a state of dismay or completely frozen. I remember
hearing a person say the phrase "being frozen to death." Fear is
the weapon of the devil. When such fear occurs, just call upon
the Holy Name of Jesus. All Bibles contain the First Letter of
Saint John. It states, "Beloved, do not believe every spirit, but test
the spirits to see whether they are from God: because many false
prophets have gone out into the world. By this you know the spirit

4   Kieran Kavanaugh and Otilio Rodriguez (Trans.), *The Collected Works of
Saint Teresa of Avila*, Vol. 2 (Washington, DC: Institute of Carmelite Studies
Publications, 1980), 406.

5   Kieran Kavanaugh and Otilio Rodriguez (Trans.), *The Collected Works of
Saint Teresa of Avila*, Vol. 2 (Washington, DC: Institute of Carmelite Studies
Publications, 1980), 416–417.

of God: every spirit that confesses that Jesus Christ had come in the flesh is from God" (1 John 4:1–2).

Evil is cunning, but this question will force it to reveal itself. Evil is so undermining that it can appear as a holy angel or even quote the Bible. So test all spirits who have come in the flesh, and rebuke them in the Holy Name of Jesus Christ to see if they are evil sources.

God allows visitations for the following reasons.

- Visits from a loved one are allowed out of love.
- A message is to be given. I met an elderly person who shared with me that when she was severely ill, her departed relative, who appeared in regular human form with regular clothes, visited her and told her exactly what to do to get well. She followed her relative's instructions and, after a few days, was totally recovered.
- The soul or spirit wants help and is in need of prayers. Only the living can help the dead with prayer. As God receives a prayer, the soul is helped, and its appearance becomes normal and is seen to be happy. The Holy Sacrifice of the Mass is the highest form of help to a soul. This is the greatest solace and support to all souls, especially for the souls of those who have committed suicide.

Shouldn't all the living be praying for the dead who want spiritual help to move toward God? And as souls of light get closer to God, they, in turn, can ask the Almighty to help us, the living, on earth. Visitations and visions can occur simultaneously.

4. **Bilocation:** Padre Pio, as seen in the book *Padre Pio: The Stigmatist* by Carty,[6] had the gift of bilocation, among others. And as all gifts should be used, he used his gifts to glorify God by helping souls. Bilocation, or being in two places at one time, covers no distance or time, as it exists in the present. It is the separation of the spirit from the body yet remaining in a total state of existence as one

---

[6] Charles Mortimer Carty, *Padre Pio: The Stigmatist* (St. Paul, MN: Radio Replies Press, 1963).

entity. A gift beyond the natural can destroy a person if it is not used to help a soul move toward God.

5. **Voices and sensible sound:** Again, as in other confrontations, there is calmness yet urgency in voices and sensible sound. Leave it in God's hands. He will show you what to make of it. Remember what John the Apostle said about how to test all souls.

Why Test the Spirits?

According to Saint John of the Cross, for every good spiritual confrontation, God will permit an evil one. This is in the soul's struggle to overcome obstacles and get strengthened.[7]

Once again, for every good vision, one must walk through hell. Hence, do not wish or want for a vision. Let it be God's will. As a reminder, Saint John's Letter tells us to test all spirits ("Did Jesus Christ come in the flesh?"). The spirit who admits that Jesus Christ has come in the flesh is of God. If the spirit gives no acknowledgment in any form, rebuke it in the Holy Name of Jesus Christ. How then do we know that something other than good exists?

Hell

Saint Teresa of Avila describes hell as a "long and narrow alleyway, low dark and confined, foul stench and swarming with putrid vermin. It is the soul itself that tears itself to pieces … that interior fire and despair, in addition to extreme torments and pains … without end, never ceasing."[8] I met a friend who could stand in a cemetery and point out graves whose souls smelled of a foul stench. These souls would be helped to God if it was God's will. Some people are gifted and guided by God to carry out this mission while on earth.

This reminded me of many readings from long ago and of people sharing with me that they believe that hell is here on earth. All the seven capital sins are bloated in humans, and when death comes, there is the grave—a hole in the ground. And the First Letter of Saint John always

---

[7]   Kieran Kavanaugh and Otilio Rodriguez (Trans.), *The Collected Works of Saint Teresa of Avila*, Vol. 2 (Washington, DC: Institute of Carmelite Studies Publications, 1980), 384.

[8]   Ibid., 213.

brings to light that Jesus Christ has come in the flesh to open the gates of hell. There is no hell with Jesus, the Son of our Heavenly Father.

The three children at Fatima also give an account of hell. When our lady stretched out her hands, "All at once the ground vanished, and the children found themselves standing on the brink of a sea of fire. ... The terrified youngsters saw huge numbers of devils or fallen angels and damned souls, demons, or fallen humans. The devils resembled hideous black animals, each filling the air with despairing shrieks. The damned souls were in their human bodies and seemed to be brown in color, tumbling about ... in the flames and screaming with terror. All were on fire within and without their bodies ... neither devils nor damned souls seemed able to control their movements ... There was never an instant's peace or freedom from pain." Our lady mentions that more souls are in hell due to the sins of the flesh. Prayers were and are asked for by the souls in hell.[9]

These accounts are similar in description. Fatima's message mentions two entities: devils (fallen angels) and demons (fallen humans).

How Can You Detect the Presence of Evil?

Nine identifying marks of evil spirits are as follows.

1. **Denial of God the Father's Plan:** When no acknowledgment is given to Saint John the Young Apostle's question "Did Jesus Christ come in the flesh?" to the living and the departed, an atmosphere of ugliness is felt.
2. **Dark Hole:** Being trapped, distortion of goodness, and torment are other aspects of negativity. A living soul can get trapped in the dark hole of self-pity, or severe depression. Look for the light, and move out; the sooner, the better. Suicidal victims need a light to show them the way. Prayers and Holy Masses, can really help these souls, especially when they realize they can no longer solve the problems they had while on earth.
3. **Hot to cold, or vice versa:** Severe temperature changes may occur in seconds. These changes may be physically felt or seen

---

9   Fintan G. Walker, "Our Lady of Fatima's Peace Plan from Heaven," Abbey Press Pamphlet #11089 (January 1950): 6–7, 12.

among humans through perceptions of the spirit, the intellect, or
something else.

4. **Stench and sulfur:** Evil's presence may be accompanied by the
actual smell of sulfur from within the earth. The senses can feel
its presence, or the circumstances of one's goodness can be twisted
out of its state of goodness in secret from others. Psychology can
be an excuse here.

5. **Fear:** Evil may be accompanied by sensible sound; its actual
presence is felt through uneasiness, ugliness, or fear itself. Saint
John of the Cross describes it as the soul being disturbed by
the presence of evil; horror seizes upon it. "This horrendous
communication proceeds from spirit to spirit manifestly and
somewhat incorporeally ... transcends all sensory pain. This
spiritual suffering does not last long, for if it did the soul would
depart from the body due to this violent communication. This
experience remains in the soul's memory and causes great
suffering."[10] Hence the phrase "frozen to death."

It is truly a spirit-to-spirit confrontation. I would like to make it
explicit that this type of confrontation is of an unearthly nature
and so frightening that it can stop all involuntary bodily functions.
Call on Jesus immediately with your mind or spirit.

What about fear as a result of inhumane treatment of others
through threats, pressure, conniving behavior, manipulation,
jealousy, or succumbing to power in order to survive? A soul, no
doubt, may lose its identity if the will, intellect, and soul give in
entirely. Psychology and psychiatry have their place for human
behavior. Individuals' spiritual aspects, psychology, and psychiatry
can join together to assist the forerunners in this area—mystics,
ministers, priests, spiritualists, and reverends. There is a fine line
between multiple personalities and possession.

6. **Black cloud or black hue:** Darkness of the mind, or plurality of
blaming, as well as black shadows or even black lightning may be
seen by human eyes. They are the opposite of the beauty of black.

---

[10]   Kieran Kavanaugh and Otilio Rodriguez (Trans.), *The Collected Works of
Saint Teresa of Avila*, Vol. 2 (Washington, DC: Institute of Carmelite Studies
Publications, 1980), 385.

This is similar to negative white, the opposite of the beauty of white. Ancient prayers relate to deliverance from lightning. More than forty years ago, I came across a prayer asking God to free us from lightning (curses) and damnation to hell.

Religious reasoning will direct the intellect to strengthen its faith in the Lord in order to handle what is about to occur. Faith does not have to be separated from the intellect, but rather, it can be its driving force.

On the human level, it results in a stubborn atmosphere of blindness to the truth, and all energy expenditures to bring the truth out are continuously blocked by a stubborn force. Constant blaming of others occurs due to the blindness, and the truth remains hidden. This could be seen in cultural pride, where suffering continues, and when church is against church. One must remember that there is always a common truth factor to agree on, no matter how many disagreements may exist. This can bring about peace.

7. **Lack of dignity:** A lack of dignity is unbalanced in the mind and disheveled in appearance.

8. **Noise, unrest, loud**: Unnecessary loudness, thrashing behavior and the like emits from the individual. There is no calmness or peace.

9. **Abuse of drugs:** Abuse of drugs, especially ice or crystal meth, effectively paralyzes the will with the sole purpose of preventing one from choosing good. Fear—whether manifested through hallucinations, uncontrollable morbid thoughts, phobias, or voices—wipes out the conscience or turns it inside out so good becomes evil and evil becomes good in the soul's eyes. The mind warps. Fear distorts the soul; it causes blindness of the soul. Drug abuse not only affects the body but also the mind, the personality or psychology of a person, and the soul.

   Research has also shown that marijuana and alcohol abuse have a tendency to release schizophrenia in individuals. What an easy way for possession to take place, let alone crime.

One needs only to read the gospels of the Holy Bible to see many of these cases.

How Can You Gain Strength in Dealing with Evil?

Ephesians 6:10–17 says, "Draw your strength from the Lord. Put on the armor of God. Our battle is not against human forces but against the principalities and powers, the rulers of this world of darkness, the evil spirits in regions above. Put on the armor of God … truth as the belt around your waist, justice as your breastplate, and zeal to propagate the gospel of peace as your footgear. Hold faith up before you as your shield; it will help you extinguish the fiery darts of the evil one. Take the helmet of salvation and the sword of the spirit, the word of God."

The following are six things to help you deal with evil.

1. **The Holy Name of Jesus Christ:** Rebuke evil only in His Holy Name. Command the demons or devils to go in the name of Jesus. In the Holy Name of Jesus Christ of Nazareth, I command you to leave immediately! Humans have absolutely no power of their own. Thus, the Holy Name of Jesus Christ should always be revered and used in holiness and not in swearing or using it lightly.
2. **The crucifix:** Rebuke the evil spirit in the Holy Name of Jesus, and hold the crucifix facing the direction of the presence of the ugly one. Saint Teresa of Avila found that it must leave. Devils fear and tremble at the sight of a crucifix. Should it be removed, they may return.
3. **Holy water:** This is always used by a priest when blessing a home. Saint Teresa of Avila also found that holy water disperses evil spirits immediately and they never return.[11] Isn't this interesting, Lou?
4. **The sign of the cross:** As many Christians are aware, this signifies the blessed Holy Trinity: the Father, Son, and Holy Spirit. We know that this is done with the actual movement of our hand and our praying to God. Especially when a spirit confronts another spirit, our spirit calls out from its spiritual side. This is the same as calling out to Jesus Christ. Someone shared with me how several people have used the sign of the cross to dispel evil. There is an account of a monk who made the sign of the cross over a youth

---

[11] Kieran Kavanaugh and Otilio Rodriguez (Trans.), *The Collected Works of Saint Teresa of Avila*, Vol. 2 (Washington, DC: Institute of Carmelite Studies Publications, 1980), 204.

whose features were distorted and, through the grace of God, was able to bring the features back to normal. Now, Lou, I really don't know how distorted the features were, but it was written that they were really bad.

5. **Standing fast against fear:** We know through life experiences and psychology that when emotions take the lead, we are unable to think clearly or see the truth. Ask our holy mother, Mary Immaculate, for help. Pray to Saint Michael, the archangel, to defend us in battle against the wickedness and snares of the devil, and by the power of God, cast the evil into hell. It has been said that the holy mother of Jesus Christ and Saint Michael, the archangel, battle evil!

Stand fast with fortitude, and do not give in to any fear. I call this stance "taking on holy anger." Be angry in holiness for God, and after you face it head-on with holy anger, the evil must immediately leave. I have learned this by articulating it with other spiritual people and experiencing it myself.

From reading *Autobiography of St. Teresa of Lisieux* by Ronald Knox,[12] I have learned that evil tries to make you subordinate through fear. It attempts to freeze you by stopping your flow of energy with God. As such, the emotions give in to fear, and your conscience is unable to function in connection with your intellect, thereby severing your connection and ties with God. Fear then takes the lead—anything to trick you into giving in to evil. Lou, this is what you were referring to.

6. **Words of Jesus (Luke 8:41–55):** "Talitha cumi," or "Maid, arise." There are also other words that Christ used to dispel negativity. In *A History of Ethiopia: Nubia and Abyssinia* (volume 1) by Sir E. A. Wallis Budge,[13] Jesus Christ is depicted as confronting the evil eye and dispelling it with two words: "Asparaspes" and "Askoraskis." Lou, souls with spiritual confrontations must do the same as you went through in the stages of healing for your PTSD and

---

12   Ronald Knox (Trans.), *Autobiography of St. Teresa of Lisieux* (New York: P. J. Kennedy and Sons, 1958).

13   E. A. Wallis Budge, *A History of Ethiopia: Nubia and Abyssinia*, Vol. 1 (London: Methuen, 1928).

alcoholism. Faith and knowledge are so important. Like you, I, too, had to rely on the goodness of others to share their journeys, but in the spiritual realm. Let me share with you other ways souls can help themselves in their healing process. Remember, now, all that I share I learned from others to whom God directed me.

Self-Help for Souls
The following are five methods for self-help for the soul.

1. **The Holy Sacrifice of the Mass:** Especially in the Holy Eucharist, the body and the blood of our Lord, Jesus Christ (the price of love that Jesus Christ paid to ransom us), are so sacred. Receive our Lord daily if possible. What strength there is to be in full possession of Jesus Christ physically and spiritually. Remember, every time we receive Him, sins are forgiven—ours as well as the sins of those for whom we pray, the living and the dead. Jesus promised this to us when He said to "Do this in remembrance of Me" (Luke 22:19 NASB). Masses help the living and the dead. Whenever a person dies, the Holy Sacrifice of the Mass is the greatest gift a living person can give to the deceased.

2. **Spiritual nourishment in prayers, actions, and readings:** As the body needs daily nourishment through food, so does the soul need daily nourishment with faith. Prayers—such acts of faith, hope, and charity; spiritual and corporeal works of mercy; and beatitudes. According to Matthew 5:1–12, faith without works is of no benefit. Reading the Holy Scripture, or Bible, reading materials on spiritual growth or self-growth, psychological reading, and reading stories on the saints help provide nourishment for the soul.

3. **Devotions:** There are many patterns of prayers, some in a litany format, in a novena 9 count, attending the Holy Hour at Church-being in the true presence of the Lord, saying chaplet prayers to the Holy Trinity, doing prayer devotions to the Sacred Heart of Jesus and the Immaculate Heart of Mary, and saying the rosary and praying to the saints and angels. These increase one's relationship with God. They involve faith, action, and especially *love*.

4. **Holy objects:** Let it be clear that one does not worship these objects. These are like having pictures of family members—reminders or representations of one's relationship with God the Most Powerful. Among these objects are statues, medals, holy pictures, and the scapular of Our Lady of Mount Carmel. When blessed, some of these have been used to rebuke evil immediately. Some have been used in exorcism. Why? Maybe because they represent God, the Father, the Son, and the Holy Spirit. And when blessed with holy water, they get enveloped in God's blessings. Evil is reminded through these objects that only God shall they worship.

5. **Conversations with others who are close to God and willing to share their experiences:** I have found so many people with much to share—so many who traveled the road like you and me—Christians helping Christians, ordinary men and women, and religious ministers from all Christian denominations. As crazy as the conversations may sound to others who do not experience such, for those who are seeking God, such articulation is not so. Rather, these conversations enrich souls to move forward.

I highly recommend that after reading the most important book, the Bible, you who are spiritual warriors and fighters read *Spiritual Warfare* by Richard Ing.[14] It is a clear, dynamic book on how to handle evil situations and wars of spirituality. It even gives insights to nonwarriors.

Live a normal life, with its ups and downs and with the limitations of your humanness. If you falter in life or fall unintentionally, pick up your cross, and continue on as Christ did. Remember, Christ fell three times, so always get up, and keep on fulfilling the will of God the Father. Live for our Heavenly Father. Our reward is not of this life but of the next.

Lou, if God be willing, others may write also in order to help other souls.

Until we meet again, peace be unto you.

---

[14]   Richard Ing, *Spiritual Warfare* (Springdale, PA: Whitaker House, 1996).

BIBLIOGRAPHY

1. Majority of all Christian Bibles
2. The Little Red Book, Hazelden Educational Materials, Center City, Minnesota, 5512-0176, pages 39, 62, 63.
3. Kavanaugh, Kieran, and Rodiguez, Otilio. The Collected Works of St. Teresa of Avila, Vol. two, Washington, D.C.: ICS Publications, Institute of Carmelite   Studies, 1980, p. 406.
4. Ibid, pp. 416-417.
5. Kavanaugh, Kieran, and Rodiguez, Otilio. The Collected Works of St. John Of The Cross, Washinton D.C.: ICS Publications, Institute of Carmelite Studies, 1979, p. 384.
6. Kavanaugh, Kieran, and Rodiguez, Otilio. The Collected Works of St. Teresa of Avila, Vol. one. Washington, D.C.: ICS Publications, Institute of Carmelite Studies, 1976, p. 213.
7. Abbey Press Pamphlet #11089, "Our Lady of Fatima's Peace Plan from Heaven," 15 January, 1950: pp.6-7, 12.
8. Kavanaugh, Kieran, and Rodriguez, Otilio. The Collected Works of St. John Of The Cross, Washington, D.C.: ICS Publications, Institute of Carmelite Studies, 1979, p. 385.
9. Kavanaugh, Kieran, and Rodriguez, Otilio. The Collected Works of St. Teresa of Avila, Vol. one, Washington D.C.: ICS Publications, Institute of Carmelite Studies, 1976, p. 204.
10. Ing, Richard. Spiritual Warfare, Whitaker House, 1996.

Edwards Brothers Malloy
Oxnard, CA USA
March 21, 2016